Kitty Cats and Crime - A Norwegian Forest Cat Café Cozy Mystery – Book 6

by

Jinty James

Kitty Cats and Crime – A Norwegian Forest Cat Café Cozy Mystery – Book 6

by

Jinty James

ISBN: 9798624342804

DEDICATION

For Annie and AJ

CHAPTER 1

"Look at my peacock!"

Lauren Crenshaw glanced over at her cousin. Zoe pointed to the fancy design she'd created on the surface of a large latte.

"That looks great." Lauren smiled.

"All ready for Ms. Tobin." Zoe grinned, picked up the tray, and headed toward the Norwegian Forest Cat Café's fussiest customer, seated at one of the pine tables.

On this Wednesday morning in late April, Annie, a large Norwegian Forest Cat for whom the café in Gold Leaf Valley, Northern California, had been named, snoozed in her pink cat bed, taking a rest from her usual duty of seating the customers.

A loud growling sound made Lauren blink. Zoe stopped on her way back from Ms. Tobin's table, and halted.

"What's that?" She frowned.

Chug chug, grr grr.

"Brrt?" Annie lifted up her head, shook herself, and jumped down from her basket. She trotted to the counter and looked up at Lauren. "Brrt?"

"I don't know what it is, Annie," Lauren replied. It sounded like the noise came from outside.

"Whatever it is, it's loud." Zoe winced as another grumble filled the air. "I'm going to have a look." She marched to the entrance door, yanked it open, and froze. "Lauren, you'd better come quick!"

"What is it?" Lauren raced around the counter and joined her cousin. She sucked in a deep breath. "Oh, no!"

Right outside their café idled a bright pink truck. The word *Cupcakes* was emblazoned on the side numerous times, in bold, gold lettering.

The serving hatch slid open and a guy in his late twenties stuck his head out of the space.

"Get your cupcakes right here! Amazing cupcakes for everyone!" He grinned. His spiky blonde hair was gelled back, and he wore fashionable stubble. His gaze met Lauren's and he winked.

"That's right, ladies, come and get some!"

"Brrt?!" Annie padded to the door, seeming to take in the scene, her green eyes wide.

"Exactly," Zoe told her. "What on earth is going on?"

"We'd better find out." Lauren stepped out onto the street. "Stay inside, Annie." She turned back to glance at the cat.

"Brrt." Annie's lower lip jutted out a tad.

"You're in charge in there while we're out here." Zoe waved a hand toward Ms. Tobin, sipping her latte and seeming not to notice the commotion outside.

"Brrp." Annie sounded a little happier, but didn't stray from her position next to the front door.

"You can't sell cupcakes here!" Zoe charged up to the truck.

"Our café is right there." Lauren pointed to their shop, just in case it wasn't obvious. "We sell cupcakes. And coffee."

"That's right," Zoe told the stranger. "And Lauren's cupcakes are awesome!"

"I'm sure there's enough business to go around." The blonde guy smirked. "My cupcakes are awesome, too."

"We'll see about that," Zoe muttered, giving him a death glare.

"What's with the cat?" The guy pointed to their café. Annie stood near the door, as if guarding the coffee shop.

"She's my cat. She seats our customers," Lauren replied.

"That's a good trick."

Lauren wished she hadn't given him that much information. Her first impression of this guy was not a good one. She didn't know whether it was because she was upset over his sudden arrival or scared he was going to steal their customers, but there was just something about him that didn't appeal to her.

He wore a gold t-shirt that enhanced his tanned, well-muscled arms, and then she noticed something that made her eyes flare.

He had a tattoo on his arm.

A portrait of a man's face.

She glanced from his arm to his countenance, and back again. And did a double take.

The portrait was of himself!

"Yeah, I get that a lot." He grinned at Lauren, flexing his arm, the sketch of his face seeming to wink at her. "The ladies love it."

"What?" Zoe nudged her, looking at her inquisitively.

"I'll tell you later," Lauren whispered.

"I don't think it's legal for you to be here," Lauren told him politely. She'd never seen another truck operating like this on the road.

"Legal schmeagle." He shrugged.

"You're blocking the road." Zoe gestured to the two-lane road.

"But street parking's allowed, isn't it?"

They looked at each other. He had them there.

"But you're touting for business." Zoe glared at him. "That's not parking, that's – that's – loitering!"

"I think I'll wait until someone with more authority tells me to move on. Not two café girls." He shook his head, as if their assertiveness amused him.

Zoe opened her mouth to speak, but Lauren gave her a warning glance. "Let's get back."

He disappeared from the serving hatch. The *chug chug* of the engine stopped.

"I'm not loitering now." He grinned at them in satisfaction. "I'm legally parked."

"Ooh!" Zoe looked like she wanted to stamp her foot.

"Don't you want to try one of my cupcakes?" he asked. "They're real good!"

Lauren scanned the hand-scrawled list taped to the side of the truck. Chocolate, red velvet, and strawberry. His prices were practically the same as hers. But she couldn't see any cupcakes out on the counter.

"Do you serve coffee as well?" she asked.

"Nah." He shook his head. "I've heard your coffee is good, so I didn't want to compete."

"But you're competing with our – Lauren's – cupcakes," Zoe pointed out.

"Even I know making a good latte can be an art." He shrugged. "But I don't see what the big deal is about making cupcakes. Anyone can do it."

"Anyone?" Zoe's eyes flared. "What do you mean, anyone?"

Lauren baked all the cupcakes, and made the batter and frosting from scratch every day. Zoe didn't have the same cupcake making flair that Lauren possessed.

"Just what I said." He smirked again, seeming to enjoy her reaction. "They're easy to make."

"Ooh!" Zoe stomped back to the café. Lauren followed her.

"What was all that about, girls?" Ms. Tobin inquired as they re-entered the café. Ms. Tobin used to be their prickliest customer, but after they had warned her she was being scammed online, Ms. Tobin had mellowed a little. Annie jumped up on the chair next to her.

"I think we've got a cupcake rival," Lauren said glumly.

"And we don't even know his name." Zoe planted her hands on her hips. "Unless it's Mr. Smirky."

***

The cupcake truck remained outside for the rest of the day. So did a lot of their customers.

"I can see them," Zoe huffed that afternoon, her nose almost pressed against the window. "They're going up to the truck and buying cupcakes – and – and – eating them!"

"Maybe he's giving them away," Lauren said hopefully. "Free samples." She didn't like to think that her customers were disloyal. On the other hand, they had a right to eat whatever they liked – from whomever they liked. Even if she didn't like it.

"I just saw money change hands!" Zoe made it sound like the worst possible crime.

"At this rate there'll be cupcakes for our dinner tonight." Lauren tried to look on the bright side. But too many cupcakes wouldn't do her curves any good. She'd vowed to improve her fitness earlier that year, but apart from taking a few more walks at lunchtime when she was able, she hadn't gotten very far.

“Goody!” Zoe grinned, but Lauren noticed that for once it didn’t reach her eyes.

Ed came out of the kitchen – a rare occurrence. He was their pastry chef, with monster rolling pins for arms, and made light, flaky Danish that everyone raved about.

“Want me to take care of him, Lauren?” he asked gruffly, his short auburn hair sticking up in tufts.

“Um … not yet,” she replied.

“Her police detective boyfriend can do that,” Zoe said. It didn’t sound like a joke.

“But thanks, Ed.” Lauren smiled at him.

“Let me know.” He nodded to both of them, vanishing into the kitchen.

“Maybe Annie and AJ can take care of him – Smirky.” Zoe jerked her head toward the street.

AJ was an eight-month-old brown tabby Maine Coon cat that Annie had found the previous year. She now resided with Ed, or was it the other way around? Lauren knew AJ had him wrapped around her little paw.

"Have you called Mitch and told him we've got a problem?" Zoe pointed to the pink van parked outside.

"No."

"Why not?" Zoe glanced around the empty café, the pale yellow walls and pine tables and chairs looking lonely. "That guy's only been here one day and already he's stealing our customers."

"At least he's not selling Danish pastries," Lauren pointed out. "Our customers should still come in for Ed's baking."

"And our coffee." Zoe sounded a little cheerier. "He said he wasn't making coffee and everyone knows that your lattes are the best!"

"So are yours," Lauren said loyally. Last year they'd taken an advanced latte art class and after practicing a lot, they could both pull off an excellent peacock or swan, as well as the usual array of hearts, tulips, and rosettas. They used great quality beans and were experts at foaming milk.

She had already told Zoe about the tattoo she'd spied on the newcomer's arm. Zoe's face had registered shocked awe at the revelation. "I'm going to have to see that for myself," she'd vowed. "I can't believe I missed it!"

Now, Lauren scanned the empty tables. Annie sat in her cat bed, her ears pricked and her eyes alert, ready for their next customer.

The entrance door opened. Lauren and Zoe turned to see who it was.

"Hi, Lauren, and Zoe." Father Mike, from the local Episcopalian church, entered the shop. Balding, of medium height and build, he was a popular member of the community.

"Brrt!" Annie ran to greet the priest.

"Hi, Annie." He bent down to greet her. "Why the long faces?" He stood as he addressed Lauren and Zoe.

"We've got competition." Lauren explained.

"And he's stealing all our customers." Zoe scowled.

"I'm sure once the novelty wears off everyone will be back to enjoy your cupcakes," he told them. "Your baking is wonderful, Lauren, and everyone around here knows it."

"Thank you." She smiled.

"You've also got Ed's pastries, and your coffee. I'm sure there's no need to worry."

"I hope not," Zoe said.

"What can we get you, Father?" Lauren asked.

"I'd love a cappuccino and a raspberry swirl cupcake."

"Coming right up," Lauren replied.

"Where should I sit, Annie?" he asked the cat.

"Brrt." Annie led him to the table nearest the window. "Brrt." *Sit here.*

"Good thinking, Annie." Zoe beamed at the silver-gray tabby.

Annie seemed to smile back at Zoe before hopping on the opposite chair to the priest's.

"Ha! Mr. Smirky doesn't have a gorgeous cat like you with him, Annie." Satisfaction crossed Zoe's face.

Annie and Father Mike 'conversed' as Lauren made the coffee and Zoe plated the cupcake. The priest told Annie about the latest church service, and she replied in a series of brrps and brrts.

They brought the order to Father Mike and chatted with him for a few minutes, before leaving him to enjoy his treats and Annie's company.

"Now what should we do?" Zoe furrowed her brow. "Father Mike is our only customer."

"Want to take a break?" Lauren suggested. "I can take care of things here."

"I feel like I've been taking a break nearly all day," Zoe grumbled. She scowled in the direction of the pink van. "I think you should call Mitch and have Smirky taken care of."

Before Lauren could answer, the door opened and two women walked in, carrying garish pink paper bags.

"Okay if we sit here and eat our cupcakes?" one of them asked, plonking herself down at an empty table and ripping open the bag.

Lauren stared at her. So did Zoe.

"Brrt?" Annie turned her head from her seat at Father Mike's table to look at them in a scolding manner.

The two women were strangers to Lauren.

After a second, Zoe found her voice.

"No, it is not okay. Not unless you order a beverage. This is a café. Not a public park."

"Sorry," the other woman said. She gave them an embarrassed smile. "I told you it wouldn't be all right," she hissed to her friend.

"Okay, sure." The first woman shrugged. "I'll have a latte."

"I'll have the same," her friend added.

"All right, then." Zoe slid off the stool behind the counter and started grinding the beans, the scent of hazelnut and spice filling the air. "I've got this," she murmured to Lauren.

"Okay." Lauren sat back down on her stool.

Annie kept an eye on the two women from Father Mike's table.

Rip!

The other woman opened her paper bag containing a cupcake.

Lauren's gaze was riveted to the concoction. A large wobbly swirl of chocolate frosting decorated the top of the cake. Colorful sprinkles, white and pink mini marshmallows, and silver sugar pearls festooned every speck of the frosting.

"Wow!" The woman who had barged into the café and plonked herself down looked at her friend's cupcake in admiration. "Mine's the same. Look!" She pulled out the cake from the pink bag.

Indeed it was. More wobbly chocolate frosting, the edible decorations crammed in every direction on top.

Zoe paused in foaming the milk, her eyes wide.

"That's a sugar explosion waiting to happen," she muttered to Lauren.

"I know." Lauren couldn't believe what she was seeing. She would have been a little embarrassed to serve something so over the top, but the two women didn't seem to mind how sugary sweet their cupcakes looked; instead they seemed to revel in it. Was there a new cupcake trend she'd missed?

"That guy is so cute." The first woman laughed. "I wouldn't kick him out of bed for eating cupcakes."

"I know what you mean." Her friend smiled, then bit into the cake. Her eyes widened as she munched. "OMG. So *sweeeet.*"

"Let me try." The first woman stuffed her cupcake into her mouth. "Mmm. Mmm. Mmm."

"Two large lattes." Zoe marched over with their order. "You can pay at the counter when you're ready to leave."

Lauren frowned at her cousin's curtness. She wasn't a fan of these two strangers, but they were paying customers – at least now. But the women seemed too engrossed in tasting their treats to notice Zoe's tone.

"Yeah, thanks." The pushy woman nodded as Zoe set the coffees down, with only a standard heart design on the microfoam, instead of Zoe's usual more advanced art.

"They don't deserve a peacock," Zoe whispered to Lauren when she returned to the counter.

"Do you really think those cupcakes taste that good?" Lauren asked her in an answering whisper. She cast her gaze down to the glass cases she sat behind. Raspberry swirl, orange poppyseed, and vanilla cupcakes filled the space, with elegant frosting and subtle decorations on top, as well as Ed's apricot, and apple Danishes.

"They can't be," Zoe murmured fiercely. "Everyone knows yours are the best."

"Thanks." Lauren smiled at her cousin. "But what about—"

The door swung open and Mitch strode in.

"Whoa," the pushy woman said, the cupcake halfway to her mouth. "Who's he?" She eyed the tall, dark-haired man in his early thirties.

"What's going on?" Mitch asked as he reached the counter. His lean, muscular frame was encased in charcoal slacks and a gray button-down shirt.

"About time you got here," Zoe told him.

"Zoe!" Lauren admonished her.

"Sorry," Zoe apologized, "but that guy out there—" she pointed to the street "—is stealing all our customers!"

"Why didn't you call me, Lauren?" Mitch asked, his brow furrowing.

"I know you're busy," Lauren said. "But what can you do? Is he committing a crime by parking outside and selling cupcakes?" She hoped he was.

"Yes," Mitch replied shortly. "He's touting for business, using street parking without a permit. I'll tell him to move on."

"Thanks," Lauren replied, touching the gold letter L necklace he'd given her. Sometimes she still had to pinch herself that Detective Mitch Denman was her boyfriend. They'd been dating for a while now and it was becoming serious.

Mitch went outside. Lauren and Zoe watched from the window. So did Annie and Father Mike. After a short discussion, with Mitch gesturing toward the end of the street, Smirky started up the engine. *Chug chug, grr grr.* With a roar, the van took off down the road.

"Good riddance!" Zoe waved at the departing van.

"Zoe!"

"Well, it is."

The pushy woman looked up from her now empty paper bag. "He's gone?" She pouted. "That cupcake was incredible with all that frosting!"

"It was, but now my teeth ache," her friend complained. She shook her head. "Too much sugar."

"Now we can drink our lattes." The pushy woman took a gulp of hers.

"All taken care of." Mitch came back inside. "I told him he'd need a permit if he wants to operate a food truck, and I know that the members on the town council don't seem to be keen on that kind of thing around here."

"Thanks." If they didn't have an audience, Lauren would have come around the counter, stood on tiptoes, and kissed him.

"I knew you'd take care of him." Zoe grinned.

"Brrt!" Annie added. She still sat with Father Mike.

"I'm glad you were able to fix things, Mitch," the priest called.

Lauren made Mitch a latte to go and gave him a vanilla cupcake. "On the house," she murmured.

"Are we still on for tomorrow night?" he asked.

"Definitely."

"Let me know if he gives you any more trouble."

"We will," Zoe said cheerily. As soon as he left the café, she turned to Lauren. "Quick, give me your car keys."

"Why?" Lauren asked as she handed them over.

"You'll see." Zoe zipped out of the café.

A minute later, Lauren looked out of the window. Zoe maneuvered her white car into the parking space right outside the café.

"There!" Zoe re-entered the shop. "He won't be able to park outside our place again."

"Good thinking." Lauren smiled at her.

"Brrt!" Annie praised from Father Mike's table.

"I think between Mitch and Zoe, you won't have any more trouble, Lauren." Father Mike came to the counter to pay. "Thank you for a delicious coffee – and cupcake. Next time I must have one of Ed's pastries." He raised his voice. "You can't get them anywhere else and they're one of the best things I've ever eaten, along with the cupcakes here."

Lauren noticed the pushy woman glance over at the priest, seeming to listen.

"Thanks," she murmured as she handed him his change.

"Here is a big tip," he said in a loud voice, clinking silver coins into the tip jar on the counter.

"Thanks!" Zoe winked at him.

After he left, the pushy woman came to the counter.

"Tell me about Ed's pastries," she demanded. "Is he hot like the cupcake guy?"

Before Lauren could decide how to answer, Zoe took over.

"Oh, yeah." She nodded. "He's hot, all right. And his pastries are amazing. There's usually a line right outside the door, especially when he—" she leaned over the counter and whispered, "makes apricot."

"I love apricot." The pushy woman fanned herself. "Gimme three." She glanced over at her friend at their table, sipping her coffee. "No, make it four."

"Coming right up." Zoe placed the pastries into a brown paper bag. She rang up the sale, including their lattes into the total.

The woman paid without a murmur, and clinked a couple of coins into the tip jar. Lauren was sure Father Mike's helpful comments had had an effect, along with Zoe's talking up of Ed.

She knew Ed did get hot in the kitchen at times. Was Zoe deliberately giving the wrong impression such a bad thing to do? Ordinarily, Lauren would have said yes, but maybe allowances could be made just this once.

CHAPTER 2

Lauren woke up the next morning telling herself to be positive.

"Brrp?" Annie enquired as Lauren sat up in bed, yawning.

"Time to get up." Lauren smiled at the cat sitting beside her. "Hopefully the cupcake guy won't be there today – Mitch moved him on yesterday."

"Brrt," Annie replied in approval. She jumped off the bed and scampered out of the room.

"I'm coming." Lauren threw on her robe and followed Annie to the kitchen. After feeding her beef and liver, she stumbled into the shower. She loved running the café, which she'd inherited from Gramms, but sometimes she disliked the early morning starts.

After they all finished breakfast, the trio trooped through the private hallway to the café.

"I bet we get lots of customers today!" Zoe unstacked the chairs.

"I hope so." Lauren looked out of the window. Her car was still parked outside the shop, but she couldn't see a pink van anywhere. Good.

They finished getting the space ready. Ed clumped into the kitchen through the rear entrance, his heavy work boots echoing through the swinging kitchen door. A moment later, the clang of pastry tins alerted them he'd started his day's baking.

Ed wasn't much of a talker and preferred to work alone.

"All ready for our first customer!" Zoe unbolted the front door and peered out. "No smirky guy either."

Chug chug, grr grr.

"Oh, no." Lauren froze. Had she imagined the sound?

Chug chug, grr grr. Louder this time.

"What?" Zoe burst into the street. "He's back again!" Her short brunette pixie cut strands stood almost upright.

The bright pink van sailed past Lauren's car and parked right in front of it. A few seconds later, the serving hatch opened and the smirking guy stuck his head out.

"How's it going?" he asked. The big fat smile on his face told them he wasn't going to be a pushover – for anyone.

Zoe had left the entrance door open, giving Lauren a front row view.

"Brrt?" Annie jumped down from her cat bed and trotted to the door.

"Stay there, Annie." Lauren hurried over to the entrance.

Déjà vu.

"Woof!" A black and white dog with short hair and a bulldog type face stuck his head out of the hatch.

Lauren stepped onto the sidewalk, shutting the door behind her. She didn't want Annie to be so curious that she left the café on her own. Annie stuck her nose to the glass door, her green eyes wide with curiosity.

"Who is that?" Zoe demanded, pointing to the dog.

"Do you like him?" Smirky grinned, patting the dog. "His name is Sweet Boy and he's a French Bulldog. My grandpa says he's a real ladies' magnet."

"What's he doing in the van?" Lauren asked.

"He's my helper. Just like your cat helps you get customers, Sweet Boy here is going to help me. The ladies won't be able to resist him, you'll see."

"Woof!" Sweet Boy seemed to agree.

"Hi, I'm Scott." Another guy who looked around the same age as Smirky appeared at the window, holding a black instant camera. He wore blue jeans and a purple t-shirt. He had short brown hair, an open face, and a slightly crooked nose. "Jason said you girls are cool about us parking here."

"No, we are not." Zoe drew herself up to her full height of five foot seven. "*Jason—*" she threw a death glare at Smirky "—was moved on by the police yesterday. Trading in a van in street parking is illegal!"

"You didn't tell me that." Scott frowned at his friend.

"It's cool, Scott. Don't worry." Jason didn't look worried at all. "We'll do business here until we're told to move on – *by the authorities* – and then we'll just park somewhere else. I set up a page for the truck on social media last night, so we'll be able to let our customers know where we are at all times."

"As long as they *know* you're on social media," Lauren said tartly. She did not like this at all.

"Oh, yeah." For a second, Jason looked like he hadn't thought of that. He quickly recovered. "We'll tell all our customers as soon as they arrive."

"Ooh, cupcakes!" A middle-aged woman halted outside the café. She looked from Annie inside the glass door, staring out at the street and the pink van, and then glanced at the two guys at the van.

Jason smiled winningly at her.

"We've got awesome cupcakes," he told her.

"We've got cupcakes too," Lauren told the woman. She didn't know her. "And Danish pastries by Ed."

"And awesome coffee," Zoe added.

"Oh, I've heard about Ed's pastries," she replied. She glanced at Annie. "And your cute cat. But I'm really in the mood for a cupcake, and I haven't seen this van before."

"Here's our list of flavors today." Jason pointed to the hand scrawled list next to the hatch. "Raspberry, chocolate, red velvet, and carrot."

"Oh, they all sound so tempting." The woman hemmed and hawed. "Carrot! No, chocolate! No, raspberry!"

"You're going to love it," Jason promised. He pulled out a container with a tall clear lid and grabbed one of the cakes with a pair of tongs.

Lauren's eyes widened. A huge dollop of bright red frosting covered the small cake, along with squishy raspberries, their juice dripping into the bright frosting. She guessed the berries were either frozen and defrosted, or canned. She'd prided herself on always using fresh ingredients. Surely she hadn't been wrong to do so? Didn't customers care about what was in their sweet treats?

"Oh, my." The woman's eyes lit up. "Thank you." She practically snatched the bag from him.

"Check out our social media page." Jason winked at her.

"I don't do that sort of thing. But my daughter does." She brightened at the thought.

The four of them watched her hurry down the street, peeking into the pink bag.

"At least she didn't barge into the café and start eating it," Zoe whispered.

"Yes," Lauren returned glumly. When was the last time she'd had a reaction like that to one of her creations? Not for a while. Maybe it was time she upped her game.

"Ladies?" Jason smirked at them. "How about trying one of my delicious cupcakes – on the house? And you could give me one of yours to sample."

"No, thanks." Zoe answered before Lauren could. "They don't look as good as Lauren's."

Jason frowned. "They don't? Why not?"

"As if we'd tell you." Zoe tossed her head, swiveled, and stalked back to the café. Lauren followed, wondering if it had been wise to answer so quickly. She wanted to understand what was so good about their rival's cupcakes.

"Start taking photos of me," she heard Jason's voice before she entered the café.

"I blew it," Zoe mourned after she entered the café and closed the door behind them. "We should have tasted his cupcakes."

"I agree," Lauren replied.

"Sorry." Zoe looked at her apologetically. "But this has never happened to us before. Everyone loves our baked goods and coffee."

"Brrt!"

"And you, of course, Annie." Zoe bent down and stroked the silver-gray tabby. "We've got the whole package right here – so why would anyone want to try his stuff?"

"Because it's something different," Lauren replied. "And I haven't come up with a new creation for a while."

"But you've got so many flavors already," Zoe protested. "Don't forget you came up with that amazing lavender cake."

"That was in January," Lauren told her. "And now it's April. Maybe our customers are getting tired of the same old thing. The same with—" she lowered her voice "—Ed's pastries. But don't tell him that."

"No way!" Zoe shook her head. "But maybe it's easier to come up with new cupcake ideas than it is with pastries? Ed already makes honeyed walnut, blueberry, cherry, apricot, and apple."

Lauren drew in her breath as an idea hit her. "What if we call our customers when Ed bakes their favorite? His honeyed walnut pastries are very popular."

"Great idea!" Zoe beamed. "We'll phone the customers who always rave about that one and tell them we can only hold their order for a couple of hours because so many people want it. They'll skedaddle down here and BAM! We've made a sale."

"I'll ask him what he's making this morning." Lauren hurried through the swinging kitchen doors into the commercial kitchen. She'd inherited Ed along with the café, and knew he liked to work independently.

"What's up?" Ed lifted his head, turning his attention away from rolling out a large rectangle of dough.

Lauren explained their idea.

"No problem." A brief smile. "I was going to make honeyed walnut today, anyway. I'll just make a double batch instead of apple."

"You're the best. Thank you." Lauren left him to it.

"Watch out, Smirky Jason," Zoe crowed. "We're going to beat you!"

Lauren sat behind the counter and tapped her pen on her order pad. She needed to come up with some new flavor ideas. But however hard she tried, her mind was blank. It didn't help that every time she looked out of the window, another customer was being served by Jason, his friend Scott, and Sweet Boy, the dog.

She frowned. Was the dog allowed back there? Because it was a certified cat café, Annie was allowed in the café area, but she certainly wasn't allowed in the kitchen. What would the rules be for food trucks regarding pets?

Maybe she should check with the town council.

Lauren glanced out of the window. She couldn't help herself. It was like picking at a hang nail.

Her eyes widened as she saw their friend Martha push her rolling walker to the cupcake truck. In her senior years, she had curly gray hair, and liked her independence.

"Zoe!" She beckoned her cousin over.

"What?"

"Look!" She pointed at the large window.

Zoe sucked in a deep breath. "No way! The traitor!"

Through the window, Lauren could see Martha talk to Smirky Jason at the truck. Then he handed her a pink bag. Martha placed it on the seat of her walker and shuffled a few steps away. Then she sat down on the walker and opened the bag, taking a bite of what looked to be a chocolate cupcake.

Zoe charged outside. Lauren and Annie followed.

"Annie!" Lauren turned around. "Go back inside, please."

"Brrt." Annie seemed to shake her head no. The tabby was an inside cat, although she accompanied Lauren for walks as long as she wore her harness.

Lauren scooped her up and hugged her.

"All right. But only if I hold you."

"Brrt," Annie replied in a mollified tone. She nestled her cheek against Lauren's for an instant.

"Caught you!" Zoe scolded Martha.

"Whaa?" Martha mumbled around a mouthful of cupcake. The word guilty flashed across her face in red neon letters.

"How could you eat his cupcakes?" Zoe demanded.

"Fwee thample," Martha explained thickly, swallowing the treat. "I didn't ask for it, I swear."

"But you took it," Zoe replied.

"If someone's going to give me a free cupcake, I'm not going to say no."

"Brrp." Annie sounded reproachful.

"Want a ride, Annie?" Martha beamed at the cat. Annie usually loved standing on the walker seat and allowing Martha to push the contraption.

"Brrt." Annie turned her head away and snuggled her face into Lauren's chest.

Lauren stroked her, the velvet fur soft against her finger tips.

"I think she's upset," Lauren murmured.

"I'm sorry." Martha rolled up the cupcake bag, a woebegone look on her face. "It wasn't that good, anyway. I didn't even eat it all, see?" She held up the balled-up bag.

"Then you can put it in the trash," Zoe told her.

"How was the cupcake, Martha?" Jason called out from the truck.

Martha shrugged, not seeming to want to be the center of attention for once.

"Leave our customers alone, you – you – cupcake stealer!" Zoe glared at him with her hands on her hips.

Jason held up his palms. "Hey, I didn't ask her to come over to the truck."

"Ooh!" Zoe flounced to the café.

"I wouldn't have tried his cupcake if I'd known Annie and Zoe would be so upset," Martha said. "You too, Lauren. Sorry."

"I understand wanting to try something different," Lauren attempted to be fair.

"But we haven't had any customers so far this morning, and hardly any yesterday."

"I'll tell the gals down at the senior center to come to your café," Martha said. "And the cupcake guy doesn't sell coffee, so you're good there."

"Except everyone seems so enthralled with his cupcakes that they're not interested in a latte or mocha from us," Lauren replied, thinking of the way Zoe had strong-armed the two women yesterday into buying coffee, when they'd only been interested in finding somewhere to sit down and eat the treats from the truck.

"I'm sure things will pick up," Martha said sympathetically. She placed her hand sideways across her mouth and whispered, "And I'll tell my pals that his cupcakes aren't too good, anyway."

"Thanks," Lauren whispered back. "But only if it's the truth."

"It is." Martha assured her.

"Brrp?" Annie lifted her head. She was still snuggled in Lauren's arms.

"I'm sorry, Annie," Martha apologized.

"Brrp." Annie placed a paw on the senior's arm, as if patting it.

"I think we're all friends again." Lauren smiled at Martha.

"Am I welcome to come in for a hot chocolate?" Martha asked.

"Of course!"

"Brrt!"

"I'll even put in extra marshmallows for you," Zoe called from the open café door.

"Goody."

***

A couple of hours later, Lauren called their customers to let them know that Ed had just made a double batch of honeyed walnut pastries. Several people promised to be there by lunch to pick some up.

"It's working!" Zoe grinned as she ended another call. "At this rate, Ed's pastries will sell out today. Just like old times."

"But it doesn't look like my cupcakes will." Lauren gazed at the tempting array of treats in the glass case. Cinnamon crumble, vanilla, and triple chocolate ganache. She hadn't sold a single one that morning.

"We've still got the lunch rush and this afternoon." Zoe tried to cheer her up.

"There wasn't much of a rush yesterday." Now it was Lauren's turn to be glum.

"You'll see."

True to their word, customers picked up Ed's pastries. But unfortunately, on their way out of the café, they detoured to the cupcake truck.

"Look!" Lauren grabbed Zoe's arm and pointed at the window. "They're buying his cupcakes!"

"I hadn't thought of that." Zoe's eyes widened. "Now we're giving Smirky Jason extra business!"

They stared at each other. Lauren was relieved that she didn't have rent or a mortgage to pay and had a small cushion of profit so if the worst came to the worst, she could still pay Zoe's and Ed's wages. As well as her own. For a little while, anyway.

The tiny lunch rush cheered them up, but it was only a trickle compared to other days – before the cupcake truck had invaded.

"I've got an idea." Zoe grinned, for an instant looking like the zippy Zoe she'd been the day before Jason and his cupcake truck had arrived for the first time.

"What is it?"

"Brrt?" Annie called from her cat bed. She hadn't been very cheery that day either, despite making up with Martha. None of her favorite customers had come in.

"You'll see." Zoe giggled. "I'll need about fifteen minutes, though."

"No problem." Lauren looked around the now empty café.

She watched Zoe zoom through the private hallway to the cottage, wondering what her cousin was up to.

When Zoe didn't emerge, she sank back down on the stool and tried to come up with some new flavor ideas. But her mind was blank. Maybe just sitting here and forcing herself to be creative wasn't working.

A black blur from outside the café caught her eye. Frowning, she walked over to the glass plated entrance door, opened the door and stepped outside. A person clad in black, and wearing a black beret and black sunglasses, stood near the truck, as if reading the menu taped to the side of the serving hatch. Then that person stepped up and spoke to Scott, Jason's friend.

Lauren blinked as she watched the stranger hand over some money and receive a large bag in return. The clothes seemed familiar.

"No way," she breathed.

A black sweater, black pants, black sneakers – the outfit was identical – apart from the sunglasses – to the one Zoe had worn a few months ago when she'd played cat burglar.

Chris, a tall guy in his late twenties with even, attractive features, whom Zoe was dating, strode toward the café, then did a double take as he glanced at the pink truck, and the person being served.

"Zoe, is that you?"

"Vat?" The person in black turned around. "Who iz dis Zoe?" The female voice had a thick French accent.

"It is you!" He came over to her.

Lauren took a few steps towards the duo, intrigued. What on earth was Zoe up to? Surely it was her, clad in that all black ensemble.

"I haf no idee vat you are talking about." The female shook her head and attempted to walk past him.

"I know it's you." He fell in step beside her.

"Come, and you vill zee it iz not," she said dramatically, pulling him toward the café. Lauren held the door open for them, shutting it firmly behind her.

The female cast a backward glance at the pink truck through the window, but Scott was now busy serving four giggling teenage girls.

"You nearly blew my cover!" Zoe yanked off the beret and sunglasses. "I was on a mission!"

"And what would that be?" Chris asked, an amused look on his face.

"These!" She held up the large pink bag. "Lauren and I need to test them to see why everyone is buying them."

"And you couldn't do that in regular clothes?" Chris gestured to her ensemble.

"Of course not." Zoe frowned at him. "What if Scott recognized me?"

"Who's Scott?"

"The guy at the truck." She jerked her head toward the window. "I thought Smirky Jason might recognize me, even in this—" she waved a hand at her clothes "—but I didn't think Scott would. And I was right!"

"I think your French accent needs work," Chris said, stifling a smile.

"Critics." Zoe sniffed in a good-natured way. "Now, we'd better try these cupcakes before anyone catches us."

"Brrt?" Annie jumped out of her cat bed and trotted toward them, an inquiring look on her face.

"Hi, Annie." Chris bent down to pet her.

"Brrp." *Hi.*

Lauren fetched plates, and they all sat down to try the cakes.

"You can have some of mine," Zoe said to Chris.

"Thanks." He grinned at her.

Lauren wished Mitch could be here, but he was busy at work. She looked at Chris enquiringly.

“Day off,” he replied to her unspoken question. He worked as a paramedic in Sacramento. “I thought I’d stop by and see Zoe.”

“Any other time you would have been welcome.” Zoe smiled at him. She cut each cupcake into half, gave Lauren her share, and then cut her halves into a sixty-forty split. She gave Chris the forty percent pieces. “Give us your honest opinion.”

Lauren looked at the offerings. It seemed Zoe had bought one of each flavor – carrot, red velvet, chocolate, and raspberry. Each cupcake had huge, wobbly swirls of frosting with edible decorations crammed into the surface.

Lauren took a bite of raspberry. And blinked. The sweetness hit her right away, coating her teeth in an avalanche of sugary, slightly grainy frosting.

When she was actually able to taste the cake part, she frowned. Getting up, she got three glasses of water and set them out on the table.

“We might need these,” she said.

“Brrt,” Annie replied in agreement. She sat at the fourth chair, watching the three of them – and the cupcakes – with wide eyes.

"Good idea," Zoe mumbled around a mouthful of cake. She made a face and swallowed quickly. "Well, I don't think much of this chocolate flavor." Colorful sprinkles, white and pink mini marshmallows, and silver sugar pearls fell off the frosting and scattered onto her plate.

"Let me try." This time Lauren ignored the frosting and just tasted the crumb of her share of the chocolate cake. She gulped down some water. "You're right." She stared at her cousin. "You don't think – he's using a box mix, do you?"

Zoe snapped her fingers. "Hey, I bet that's it!"

"You don't think he made these himself?" Chris put down his half eaten red-velvet sample.

"What do you think?" Lauren gestured to his plate.

"Yeah, you're our male taster," Zoe told him. "Although more women than men come in here and buy Lauren's creations."

"But some of them take them home for their husbands as well," Lauren reminded her.

"True. And Mitch enjoys your cupcakes – especially vanilla," Zoe teased.

Lauren hoped the small touch of heat on her cheeks wasn't showing.

"What's your verdict?" Zoe asked Chris.

"It's okay." He shrugged.

"Okay?" Zoe narrowed her eyes. "What do you mean, 'It's okay'?"

"I mean, I guess this cupcake is okay." He motioned to the smidgen left on his plate. "It's not as good as Lauren's, that's for sure, but it's not so bad I'm going to take it back to the truck and ask for a refund if I'd bought it."

Zoe's eyes remained narrowed. "But you can taste the difference, right? Between Lauren's and Smirky Jason's?"

"Of course," Chris assured her.

All three females continued to stare at him.

"Which one would you want to buy the most?" Zoe continued to interrogate him.

"Lauren's, of course," Chris assured them.

"Good answer." Zoe sounded partly mollified.

"What did you think of the frosting?" Lauren asked him.

"Too sweet," he replied promptly.

"Hmm. You might have *just* passed the cupcake test," Zoe told him.

"Do you cupcake test all the guys you date?" Chris joked.

"Just you so far," Zoe replied.

They shared an affectionate look.

After a moment, Lauren cleared her throat.

"So why are people buying these cupcakes if they're not too good?" she asked.

"Because like you said before, they're new and different," Zoe answered promptly.

"Yeah, and the truck is right outside. They don't have to come in here and order something."

The three of them looked at Chris.

"It's not my fault people are lazy." He shook his head.

"But we've got Annie," Lauren told him.

"Brrt!" *That's right.*

"And he's got a French bulldog called Sweet Boy," Zoe said glumly.

"I'm sure once your customers try his cakes and realize they're not as good as yours, they'll come back to you," Chris said.

"I hope so," Lauren replied. "While there's still a café to come back to."

CHAPTER 3

That evening, Lauren had dinner with Mitch. They visited their favorite restaurant, a small bistro on the outskirts of Gold Leaf Valley. He listened attentively to her cupcake woes, telling her she should have called him today when the truck had returned.

"I'll take care of it if he comes back," he promised.

"Thanks." She smiled at him over their shared dessert of caramel brownie and vanilla bean ice-cream.

Lauren felt a lot better about the situation as Mitch drove her home. He'd been busy investigating a series of burglaries which had taken up a lot of his time lately, and they hadn't seen each other as much as usual.

"We should be able to close this case soon," he told her as he pulled up outside her cottage.

"Good," she said, before they kissed goodnight.

He walked her up the porch steps.

"Are Zoe and Annie spying on us tonight?" he asked.

"I don't think so. Since Zoe's been dating Chris, I think she's delegated the spying duties to Annie."

He chuckled, then kissed her tenderly once more.

"I'll try to stop by the café tomorrow," he told her.

She nodded, then let herself inside.

"Did you have a good time?" Zoe appeared in front of her in the hallway.

Lauren placed a hand on her chest, inhaling quickly. "Don't scare me like that!"

"Sorry."

"Brrp?" Annie came running from the living room. She didn't like to be left out of things.

"So you two weren't spying tonight?" Lauren asked.

"Nope." Zoe grinned. "Not this time."

***

The next morning, Friday, Zoe hummed as she slathered butter on her toast.

"It's club night at Mrs. Finch's," she mentioned to Lauren and Annie.

"Mm," Lauren mumbled around a mouthful of granola.

"Brrt!" *Yes!*

The four of them belonged to a craft club started by Zoe, but held at the house of one of their favorite customers, an elderly lady called Mrs. Finch.

Zoe had started a few different crafts, and was now keen on exploring pottery.

"I'm going to show Mrs. Finch the ashtray I made in class last week," Zoe said. "I can't wait until she sees it!"

"How is class going?" Lauren asked.

"Good."

Zoe's classes were held in Sacramento, and she usually caught up with Chris afterward, if he wasn't on duty.

Both of them had started off with knitting, which Lauren continued to do. So far, she'd made two scarves and two hats, one each for her and Mitch.

Zoe had: knitted blankets for Annie, crocheted a scarf for herself, made string-art pictures (one of which had prime wall placement in the café, depicting a pink-frosted cupcake), made bead jewelry, and was now turning lumps of clay into ashtrays.

"What are you going to do with your ashtray?" Lauren asked. "We don't smoke."

"I thought I could put it here on the table." Zoe tapped the wooden table. "For our keys."

"Good idea."

"Brrt."

They finished breakfast and left for work.

After unstacking all the chairs, Lauren started baking cupcakes, including a batch of vanilla.

On the dot of nine-thirty, they opened for customers.

"Oh, hello, Lauren." Ms. Tobin entered.

"Hi, Ms. Tobin," Lauren said cheerfully.

"Brrt!" Annie trotted over to her.

"Where should I sit, Annie dear?" the tall, slim woman in her fifties peered down at Annie.

"Brrt." *Over here.* Annie led the way to a small table near the counter.

“Lauren, I hope that cupcake fellow isn’t stealing your business.” Ms. Tobin looked around the empty café.

“I’m afraid he is,” Lauren replied glumly.

“Yeah.” Zoe popped up behind the counter.

“What can we get you?” Lauren approached their only customer.

“I have a confession to make.” Ms. Tobin looked discomfited. “I must admit, when I was at my friend’s place yesterday, she offered me one of the cupcakes—” she lowered her voice, although there wasn’t anyone else around “—from *the truck.”*

“What did you think?” Lauren asked curiously.

“It was not as good as yours, Lauren.” Ms. Tobin shook her head. “Frankly, I was surprised that my friend seemed to like them. We tried two flavors – carrot, and chocolate. I thought she had a discerning palate like my own, but now—”

“We tried them yesterday too,” Zoe confessed. “Yuck!”

"My friend raved about how good-looking the cupcake man was, and how he must have tried hard to make the frosting perfect like yours, Lauren, and how thoughtful it was of him to put so many edible decorations on top. But it was just too sugary sweet for me, I'm afraid."

"I'm glad you haven't defected, Ms. Tobin," Zoe told her.

"Brrt!" Annie sat on the opposite chair.

"Of course I would never do such a thing." Ms. Tobin smiled fondly at Annie. "The cupcake truck doesn't sell coffee, my friend told me, so I'm sure everyone will come back here. Believe me, I will never be tempted to buy anything from that truck after my sample yesterday."

"That's good to know," Lauren replied. At least they still had one loyal customer.

"Besides," Ms. Tobin added, "when I walked past the truck the first day he was here, he smirked at me. My mother told me never to trust a smirking man."

Chug chug, grr grr.

"Oh no." Lauren felt sick. "He's back!"

"Let me see." Zoe raced to the window. "Yep."

"Oh, dear." Ms. Tobin frowned. "What will you two do?"

"Call Mitch." Lauren hurried to the counter and grabbed her phone.

"Mitch said it's illegal for him to park and trade here like this." Zoe came back to Ms. Tobin's table.

"I'm glad someone is looking out for you." Ms. Tobin smiled.

"We can look out for ourselves," Zoe told her. "But it's nice to have back up."

"Brrt!" Annie agreed.

"I had to leave a message." Lauren furrowed her brow.

"That's no good." Zoe grimaced. "Maybe we should ask Ed to take care of things – he did offer."

"I know, but I don't want to have to ask him to do something like that," Lauren replied.

"Free samples!" they heard distantly from the street. "Get your free samples!"

"What?" Lauren and Zoe looked at each other.

“Call Mitch again,” Zoe urged.

Lauren did so, but his voicemail came on once more. She didn’t want to end up sounding crazy by leaving a ton of messages for him to listen to, so she ended the call without leaving another. She knew he’d get back to her as soon as he could.

“It looks like we’re on our own,” she told her cousin.

“I’m going out there.” Zoe dusted her hands together, as if getting ready for a confrontation.

“Will you be okay here by yourself, Ms. Tobin?” Lauren asked. “Ed’s in the kitchen.”

“I’ll be fine,” Ms. Tobin assured them.

“Come on.” Zoe led the way out of the café, Lauren in the middle and Annie bringing up the rear.

“Only if I hold you.” Lauren turned around, bent down, and opened her arms. Annie jumped into them and nestled in the embrace.

“What are you doing?” Zoe demanded as she neared the truck. Once again, the pink vehicle was parked just a few yards from the café, in front of Lauren’s car.

"Finding customers." Jason smirked. "It's a free country."

"Not around here it's not," Zoe informed him. "The police have already told you it's illegal to park here and do business."

He shrugged. "Then they can move me on."

"Woof!" The French bulldog appeared, his head appearing in the serving hatch, but this time he had a red collar around his neck with a large paper sign attached to it.

Lauren read the sign.

"My name is Sweet Boy. Aren't I cute?"

"Brrt?" Annie wriggled in Lauren's arms, and stretched out a paw towards Sweet Boy.

"Woof!" Sweet Boy bared his teeth.

Lauren didn't think it was a smile.

"I think Annie's trying to say hello to Sweet Boy," she told Jason.

"He doesn't like cats. He thinks this is his territory and cats don't belong here." A shark-like grin stretched across Jason's lips.

Zoe sucked in a huge breath. Lauren waited for the explosion but before her cousin could open her mouth, two twenty-something women strolled up to the truck.

"Look! Isn't he cute?" One of the women pointed at Sweet Boy. After a moment, she said in a baby voice to the dog, after reading his sign, "Yes, you are a cutesy wootsy doggy dog dog."

Somehow Sweet Boy contrived to look modest.

In a normal voice to her friend, she said, "We must buy some cupcakes!"

"Def," her friend replied.

Zoe didn't budge from her position at the truck window as the two women bought six cupcakes.

Lauren tried not to roll her eyes as Jason flirted with the pair as he filled the cupcake bag. She hadn't seen these women before. Maybe his social media campaign was working. She'd have to talk to Zoe about doing something like that to drum up business.

The two women giggled as they finally sauntered away, looking into the cupcake bag at the same time.

"See you soon," Jason called after them.

"You definitely will." The baby talk woman turned around and winked at him.

"That's it!" Zoe planted her hands on her hips. "You're deliberately taking our business away. You can't trade here!"

Jason narrowed his eyes. "Who says?"

A screech of tires caught Lauren's attention. A flashy red car screamed to a stop in front of the pink truck.

"Jason!" A slim girl in her early twenties with long, layered strawberry blonde hair rushed over to the truck, nearly pushing Zoe out of the way.

"What are you doing here, Jessica?" Jason scowled.

"I need to talk to you," Jessica replied. "Pleeease?" She looked at the dog and frowned. "What are you doing with Butch?"

"Butch?" Lauren queried. "I thought his name was Sweet Boy."

"That's his working name," Jason told her. "His real name is Butch."

"Huh?" Zoe looked puzzled.

"Don't you have work nicknames?" Jason sounded exasperated.

"No." Lauren and Zoe spoke at once.

"Brrt." *No.*

"You'll do anything to get the girls, won't you, Jason?" Jessica demanded, flicking a glance at Sweet Boy's sign. "Well, it won't work." She ignored Lauren, Zoe, and Annie. "If I can't have you, nobody can!"

"How did you know I was here?" Jason demanded.

"Scott told me."

Jason glowered at her.

"Look, babe, we broke up, okay? It's over. I can see anyone I want and you can see anyone you want. That's what it means when you break up with someone. I don't know how to make it any clearer. We're over and I never want to see you again."

Lauren's eyes widened at the brutal reply.

Zoe sucked in her breath.

"You don't mean that. You can't!" A tear rolled down Jessica's cheek.

"How many times do I have to tell you it's over?" He shook his head. "If you come near me again, I'll call the cops."

Lauren shifted uncomfortably and caught Zoe's eye. They should go back to the café so Jessica wouldn't have an audience to her humiliation.

Zoe nodded and backed away from the truck.

"But you said you loved me!" Jessica wailed.

"And now I don't," Jason replied. "Look, you're bad for business. No one's going to come over and buy a cupcake while you're making a scene. Go home. And stay away from me."

"But … but …"

"Grrrr." Sweet Boy bared his teeth in a snarl.

"Oh!" Jessica fled from the truck, running toward the café.

"Come inside." Lauren hurried to open the door for the girl.

"I can't believe he's so cruel," Jessica sobbed as she entered the shop. She sank down at the nearest table and cradled her head. The cloying scent of her rose perfume filled the air.

"Hot chocolate with lots of marshmallows," Zoe whispered to Lauren and Annie.

"Brrt!" Annie agreed as Lauren set her down. The feline hopped onto a chair at Jessica's table and peered at her.

A loud sniff. "Why is your cat looking at me?" Black streaks of mascara ran down Jessica's face.

"She's wondering why you're so upset," Lauren said gently. She glanced over at Ms. Tobin's table. The older woman's eyes were wide as she took in the scene, then she studied her coffee mug.

"I've always liked cats better than dogs," Jessica said in a watery voice. She peeked through her hands at Annie. "She's got lots of fur."

"She's a Norwegian Forest Cat," Lauren told her.

"That sounds cool." A tremulous smile. "She's very pretty."

"Her name is Annie," Lauren replied. "I'm Lauren, and this is Zoe."

"Hi, Annie." Jessica lowered her hands from her face.

"Brrp." *Hi.*

"Here's a hot chocolate for you." Zoe appeared with a steaming mug crammed full of pink and white marshmallows. "On the house."

"Thanks, Zoe." Jessica stirred the concoction, watching the marshmallows whirl around. "I try not to eat much sugar, though. Jason says – said – I have to watch it so I don't get fat."

Lauren and Zoe sucked in a breath at the same time. Jessica was on the thin side of slim.

"I don't think Jason knows what he's talking about," Lauren finally said.

"Yeah." Zoe nodded vigorously. "Plus you've broken up with him, so now you can do whatever you want."

That turned out to be the wrong thing to say.

"Why did he dump me?" Jessica wailed. Her shoulders shook and more tears leaked down her eyes. "I was so good to him! I did whatever he wanted. I even babysat Butch when his grandpa went to Vegas because Jason said he was too busy to do it!"

Lauren and Zoe exchanged a glance but it was Ms. Tobin who spoke.

“I don’t mean to eavesdrop, dear, but it sounds like you’re much better off without him.”

“Oh - oh – ohhhh!” Jessica sank her head in her hands once more.

“Brrt.” Annie hopped from the chair opposite Jessica to the one next to her. “Brrt.” She tentatively placed a paw on the girl’s arm.

“What’s she doing?” Jessica sniffed.

“I think Annie’s trying to comfort you,” Lauren replied.

“Brrt!”

“You’re such a nice girl.” Jessica gave Annie a watery smile.

Annie patted the girl’s arm once more.

“I think you need a cupcake,” Zoe told her.

Jessica shuddered. “No, thanks. Jason made me try one of his and it wasn’t very good. But I couldn’t tell him that.”

“Lauren’s cupcakes are way better,” Zoe assured her.

“You don’t have to eat one if you don’t want to,” Lauren told Jessica. “We have Danish pastries that are really good.”

“Really good? They’re totally awesome,” Zoe enthused.

"A Danish might cheer me up," Jessica replied slowly.

"Attagirl." Zoe rushed to the counter.

"I'm going to give you Ed's new creation – honeyed walnut." Zoe paused. "You can eat nuts, can't you?"

"Yes," Jessica replied.

"Good." Zoe brought over the tender, flaky pastry, baked to a golden perfection. Honey encrusted walnuts dotted the surface. "Wait until you taste this!"

Jessica broke up the pastry into small pieces and then popped one into her mouth. A moment later, she smiled.

"Did you make these?" She looked at Lauren and Zoe.

"No, Ed did," Lauren replied. "He's my pastry chef."

"But Lauren's cupcakes are just as good," Zoe said loyally. "Wait until you taste one."

"Zoe," Lauren said in a warning tone, but Zoe didn't seem to notice, bringing over a vanilla cupcake, the frosting swirled to perfection on top.

"Here." Zoe placed the cupcake in front of Jessica. "Try it."

"You don't have to," Lauren said gently.

"Maybe just a little taste." Jessica used the fork Zoe provided and scooped up a little of the frosting. "Oh, wow." She closed her eyes as she swallowed. "Mmm."

"Thanks." Lauren smiled.

Jessica dug into the cupcake, until soon there were only a few crumbs on the plate.

"I don't even feel guilty about eating sugar," she marveled.

"You shouldn't," Zoe told her. "And you won't get a sugar hangover from eating Lauren's cupcakes, either. Or Ed's pastries."

"I'd better drink my hot chocolate before it gets cold." Jessica took a large swallow. "Oh, yum!"

"Would you like to have some time by yourself with Annie?" Lauren asked tactfully. She didn't want Jessica to think they were standing over her, watching her eat.

"No, it's okay," Jessica replied. "You two – three—" she glanced at Annie "—

have been so kind. You don't even know me."

"We could see you were upset," Zoe told her.

"It's totally understandable," Lauren added, not wanting to say anything that would upset Jessica.

"We were together for six months," Jessica explained before she popped another piece of Danish into her mouth. "I believed him when he said he loved me. But lately he seemed distant, and didn't call me as much. And then my friend said she'd seen him at a club with another girl."

Lauren and Zoe exchanged a glance. Uh-oh.

"And then – and then—" she drew in a big breath "—he dumped me a few days ago – by text!"

"What a jerk," Zoe muttered.

"Who does that?" Jessica asked. "So I went over to his place, at first thinking it was a joke, but he said no, it was for real. I asked him if he'd found someone else, and he said no, and totally denied he'd been at the club that night with another girl, but I couldn't help thinking he was lying. Because there's no way my friend would have said that to me if she hadn't seen it with her own eyes."

"So you came to talk to him today?" Zoe asked.

"Yeah. I couldn't let it go. I kept thinking, what if he'd been cheating on me the whole time we were together?" Jessica swiped her eyes. "But surely I'd know, right? So then I thought, why did he dump me? I went looking for him, and couldn't find him, so I called his friend Scott. And he told me he was working the cupcake truck over here."

"That's the guy who was here yesterday working with Jason?" Lauren queried.

"I guess." Jessica shrugged. "They've been friends since kindergarten."

"So why are they selling cupcakes?" Zoe asked curiously.

"Beats me," Jessica replied. "They were both working construction, then Jason hurt his hand. It's totally better now," she added, "but I think he wanted an easier job. And then he told me he came up with this idea for a cupcake truck and how simple it would all be."

“But why is he selling them here?” Lauren asked. “Are you guys from around here?”

“Nope.” Jessica shook her head. “We’re all from Sacramento.”

“Maybe he thought it would be easier to do it here without the proper permits,” Zoe pondered. “I mean, Mitch told him to move on, but he’s come back, hasn’t he? And he hasn’t been arrested yet.” She turned to Lauren. “You should try calling Mitch again. Right now.”

“Okay.” Lauren fetched her phone. She knew Mitch would have called her the moment he’d gotten her message, if he was able to.

Lauren listened to Mitch’s voice directing her to leave a message. Ordinarily, it would give her a little thrill to hear her boyfriend’s deep, masculine voice, but at this moment she felt a frisson of frustration instead.

She was tempted to just hang up again, but decided to leave another message in case her first one hadn’t gotten through.

“He’s still not picking up?” Zoe frowned. “Maybe he’s pursuing a criminal right now and is about to slap the cuffs on him."

"Maybe you're watching too many crime shows," Lauren said mildly. She didn't want to think about Mitch being in danger. Gold Leaf Valley was usually a quiet, peaceful town, apart from the occasional murder – and burglary.

"Maybe we should march down to the town council and demand they do something about the cupcake truck," Zoe said, determination in her voice. "We don't want people to copy him and have this place turned into urban central."

"You've got a point." Lauren shoved the phone in her jeans pocket. "We could close early and go over there while the office is still open."

"Deal." Zoe grinned.

They talked to Jessica for a while longer, Zoe walking her to her car. Lauren watched the two girls totally ignore Jason, who leaned out of the serving window of the truck, seeming to take a great interest in his ex-girlfriend leaving.

"I must be off, Lauren." Ms. Tobin approached the counter, and paid for her coffee. She clinked a few coins into the tip jar.

"Thanks, Ms. Tobin." Lauren smiled goodbye.

"Brrt!" Annie added.

Zoe returned to the café after Ms. Tobin left.

"Phew!" She flopped down onto a stool behind the counter. "I had a hard time not saying anything to Smirky Jason as we walked past him."

"I think it's good that you didn't," Lauren replied.

"I just hope her next boyfriend is a whole lot better than him." Zoe jerked her thumb in the direction of the cupcake truck.

A few more people trickled in for the lunch "rush", but it was quiet around three o'clock.

"I hope Mrs. Finch is okay," Zoe said. "She hasn't been in the last few days and tonight is craft club."

"I know," Lauren replied. She'd been so caught up with the drama outside that she'd temporarily forgotten that one of their favorite customers hadn't popped in.

"Why don't we check on her on the way back from the town council?" Zoe asked.

"Good idea." Lauren nodded.

"In fact, I think we should close right now – for the rest of the day."

Lauren looked at her cousin, a trifle shocked. But then she nodded. "Why not? I can't imagine we'll get many customers in the next two hours. And Ed went home at lunch time – he asked for the afternoon off since it was so quiet."

"Let's go!" Zoe slid off the stool.

"Annie, we're closing early today," Lauren said to the cat sitting in her basket, ears pricked and green eyes alert.

"Brrt!" She scampered to the private hallway that led to the cottage, shimmied through the cat flap in the door, then wriggled through the flap at the other end.

"We'll be home soon," Lauren added.

"We're going to take care of that cupcake truck," Zoe called after her.

"Brrt!" sounded in the distance. *Good.*

Lauren and Zoe locked up and stepped out onto the sidewalk.

"Leaving early?" Jason smirked at them from the truck window.

"We're going to the town council," Zoe told him. "What you're doing is illegal and we're going to put a stop to it!" She marched down the street, away from the truck.

Lauren hurried to keep up, wondering if the look of chagrin on his face would last long.

At the town council, they were informed that the matter would be looked into – in fact, an officer would go down right now and inform Jason that he couldn't trade without a permit.

"Good!" Zoe nodded in satisfaction.

The officer drove to the café, while Lauren and Zoe walked the couple of blocks. When they arrived, the pink truck was gone. The officer got out of his car and shook his head.

"There's no truck here."

"Pooh." Zoe sounded disappointed.

"Call us if he comes back and we'll get here as quickly as we can," the officer told them, before getting back in his vehicle.

"Next stop, Mrs. Finch," Zoe declared.

"I hope she's okay," Lauren fretted as they walked around the block to the sweet, cream Victorian house the elderly lady called home. The small town dated from the Gold Rush era, and some of the houses were living proof.

A neat front lawn greeted them, bordered with orange and yellow poppies. They walked up the path and knocked on the door.

"Hello, girls." Mrs. Finch smiled at them. Her gray hair was piled on top of her head in a bun, and she wore a beige skirt with a dusty rose cardigan which seemed just right for the April weather.

She peered down, then looked disappointed. "Where's Annie? Is she all right?"

"She's fine, Mrs. Finch," Lauren replied. "We were just checking you were okay."

"That's kind of you, dear," the senior replied. "I'm sorry I haven't visited the café, but I've had a few appointments this week. You're still coming over tonight, aren't you?"

"Of course," Zoe assured her.

"Annie too," Lauren added.

"That's lovely." Mrs. Finch beamed.

They said goodbye, and walked home.

"I can't wait to show Mrs. Finch my ashtray," Zoe said. "I wonder what she'll think."

CHAPTER 4

Lauren, Zoe, and Annie enjoyed themselves that night at Mrs. Finch's house, although Lauren felt guilty she wasn't doing any actual crafting. Now that she'd finished Mitch's hat and scarf, as well as her own, she wasn't sure what to knit next.

Zoe showed Mrs. Finch her ashtray, which was duly admired – brown clay in a vaguely rectangular shape with a couple of lumpy bits.

"The instructor says I'm getting better," Zoe told them all. "I haven't shown any of you the first ashtray I made." She shuddered.

"Not even Chris?" Lauren teased gently.

"Nope." Zoe shook her head.

They told Mrs. Finch all about the cupcake truck and smirking Jason, Mrs. Finch seeming shocked at his audacity.

"I'm sorry I haven't heard anything about this, girls." She tsked. "I can't believe all your regulars have deserted you."

"Apart from Ms. Tobin," Lauren replied.

"I was surprised as well," Zoe admitted.

"People aren't always predictable," Mrs. Finch remarked.

Lauren and Zoe discussed what they could do on social media to improve business, Zoe volunteering to add some more posts to their café page.

After a pleasant evening, they said goodbye to Mrs. Finch.

"When are you seeing Chris again?" Lauren asked as they drove home.

"We haven't made a date," Zoe admitted. "He's busy working."

"But he came by the café the other day," Lauren reminded her.

"Yeah." Zoe smiled softly.

They talked about trying to come up with some new cupcake flavors for the next week the rest of the way home.

***

The next morning, Lauren woke up determined to be positive, and enjoy her days off. They closed the café at lunchtime on Saturdays and didn't re-open until Tuesday.

She had a date with Mitch that night, which was another reason to put her in a good mood.

After breakfast, the trio trooped down the hallway to the café. Ed didn't work on Saturdays. But with the way business had been this last week, there wouldn't have been any need for him to come in, anyway. Lauren decided to only bake two batches of treats this morning; lavender, and cinnamon swirl.

"Good choice," Zoe praised as she watched Lauren place the pretty cupcakes into the glass case. "I can't believe anyone would choose *his* cakes over yours."

"Thanks." Lauren smiled briefly.

Even the *chug chug, grr grr,* sound of the cupcake truck pulling up outside didn't bother her as much.

"Not again," Zoe groaned as she looked out of the window.

"We'd better open up," Lauren said.

"Okay." Zoe unbolted the front door.

"Brrt?" Annie sauntered over to the *Please Wait to be Seated* sign, as if waiting for her first customer.

"Hopefully someone will come in soon," Lauren told her.

"Brrp."

"Oh, look, it's Claire and little Molly." Zoe grinned as she pointed to the mother and daughter duo outside. Blonde-haired Claire pushed Molly in a stroller toward the café, then stopped, her attention caught by the pink truck.

"Oh no," Lauren groaned as she watched Claire approach Jason's truck.

"He's not going to steal them!" Zoe raced outside.

Lauren was a little surprised that two of their favorite customers were investigating their rival. Claire usually raved about their cupcakes and coffee, and Annie and Molly seemed fascinated with each other. Maybe she should go outside for a better look.

"Pink!" she heard blonde toddler Molly squeal as she pointed at the truck.

Lauren joined Zoe outside their café.

"You can't go over there and harangue him." Lauren placed her hand on Zoe's arm.

"I guess not." Zoe said in a disgruntled manner. "I don't want to do anything to upset Molly."

"Good." Lauren turned around to check on Annie, who stood in the doorway, watching the scene as well.

"Cino, cino," Molly chanted, continuing to point at Jason, dressed in jeans and a blue t-shirt, his blond hair gelled to perfection.

"Woof!" Sweet Boy poked his black and white head above the serving hatch. He wore his red collar but not the paper sign explaining how cute he was.

"Ooh, doggy!" Molly giggled.

"Do you make babycinos?" Claire asked Jason.

"No. What's that?" He frowned.

"It's something Lauren and Zoe make for Molly." She gestured to her daughter in the stroller.

"We don't do coffee," he informed her, "but we have the best cupcakes you'll ever try. Don't we, Sweet Boy?" He turned to the French bulldog.

"Woof!"

"Well, I don't know," Claire hesitated.

"Go on," he urged her. "I bet your daughter would like something sweet."

"I want cino!"

"They don't have your special drink here." Claire bent down to Molly. "Only Lauren and Zoe have that. But they have cupcakes. I'll give you a little of mine to try."

"O-kay," Molly said doubtfully.

"I'll try a chocolate cupcake," Claire said.

"Great choice." Jason stuffed the treat into a pink paper bag and winked at her. "These are super popular."

"Thanks." Claire paid and wheeled the stroller a short distance away, halfway between the truck and the café, seeming not to realize that Lauren, Zoe, and Annie were watching.

She tore open the bag and pinched off a small mouthful. "Here, darling." She placed the dark brown morsel into Molly's outstretched hand.

Molly stuck it in her mouth and chewed. She chewed some more. Screwing up her face, she cried, "Yucky!

Want Annie cake!" She spat out the half-eaten cake, little brown blobs dribbling down her chin. Her feet beat an angry rhythm on the stroller.

Claire looked shocked at Molly's outburst. Lauren watched her try a piece of the cupcake, frowning in concentration. After she swallowed, she shook her head.

"You're right, Molly. But Lauren makes the cupcakes, not Annie."

"No, Annie cake!" She pouted at Sweet Boy. He and Jason had been watching the scene, Jason's face impassive.

Lauren's eyes widened as Sweet Boy slowly stuck his pinky-red tongue out at the toddler. Molly gasped at the same time.

"Mommy, doggy—" but Claire had already wheeled around to face the café and apparently didn't see Sweet Boy's actions.

"Did you see what Sweet Boy just did?" Zoe muttered to Lauren.

"I must apologize." Claire wheeled to a stop outside the café door when she saw them standing there. “I shouldn’t have tried that man’s cupcakes.”

“We understand,” Lauren replied.

“Molly didn’t,” Claire said ruefully.

Lauren, Zoe, and Annie ushered in the mother and daughter, who had ceased pouting.

“Molly wants Annie’s cupcakes,” Claire told them as they all sat down at a large table. “I told her that Lauren is the one who bakes them, but she insisted on calling them Annie cakes.”

Lauren cast Annie a fond look. The silver-gray tabby sat next to Molly, allowing the little girl to give her gentle “fairy pats”. Molly beamed at the cat, her tantrum forgotten.

“Actually, Annie’s helped me mix up new creations at home,” Lauren replied.

“Annie cakes!” Molly crowed.

“Brrt!”

They all laughed.

Lauren, Zoe, and Annie spent a pleasant time with Claire and Molly. Claire’s husband had been called into the office that morning to handle a sudden crisis, so she was at a loose end. For a little while they had the café to themselves, then more customers trickled in.

"I'll never be swayed to try that man's cupcakes again." Claire gestured to the bright pink truck outside. "I'm just sorry you had to see us be tempted like that."

"Bad doggy." Molly pointed to the truck. Sweet Boy was still at the serving hatch, looking as sweet and innocent as could be, his tongue inside his mouth.

"Maybe he scared her when he barked at her," Claire said in a puzzled voice. "I thought it was just a friendly hello from him. But Molly isn't used to dogs."

"But she's used to cats." Zoe grinned.

They said goodbye to Claire and Molly.

"Should we have told her that Sweet Boy stuck his tongue out at Molly?" Lauren asked her cousin.

"Do you think she'd believe us? I wouldn't have, if I hadn't seen it with my own eyes."

CHAPTER 5

More and more customers came in that morning, until it was almost like old times.

"Hans!" Lauren came around the counter to greet one of their favorites.

"Ach, hello, Lauren." The dapper gentleman in his sixties smiled at her.

"Are you okay?" she asked. "You haven't been in recently."

"Oh, I am fine." He spoke to Lauren while bending down stiffly to pet Annie, who had scampered over to greet him. "I visited my daughter in Sacramento and stayed at her house. She said it would be too much for me to drive a two-hour round trip every day and perhaps she was right." He sighed.

"Did you have a good visit?" Lauren asked, walking beside him and Annie as the feline slowly led him to a table.

"*Ja,* it was *gut.*" He beamed, looking a little like Santa Claus in the moment, although slimmer.

"Hi, Hans!" Zoe zoomed over to them, an empty tray in her hands.

"What is going on out there?" Hans pointed to the pink truck outside. "He is selling cupcakes too?"

"Yes," Lauren and Zoe chorused.

"Brrt."

"That is no *gut.*" Hans sat down at the small table Annie had stopped at.

"Brrp." *That's right.* Annie hopped up on the chair opposite Hans.

"So far, he just seems to be getting away with it." Lauren sighed.

"Then you must do something about it," Hans told them.

"We've tried," Zoe protested.

"His cupcakes aren't very good," Lauren said in a low voice. "Zoe and I sampled them."

Zoe told Hans all about Molly's reaction to the morsel she'd eaten, making the elderly German laugh.

"But you seem quite busy right now." He gestured to the buzzing café.

"For the first time in days," Lauren told him. "I think we're going to run out of cupcakes for once."

"Then I must put my order in now," Hans said. "My daughter took me to a bakery in Sacramento, but they did not have cupcakes like yours. It was all nuts and seeds – like birdseed." He shuddered.

They sped away to the counter to fill Hans' order of a cappuccino and a lavender cupcake.

"It's a shame Ed doesn't work Saturdays," Zoe mused as she created a peacock on the surface of the microfoam.

"I know," Lauren replied. Her gaze flickered to the truck outside – no customers at all right now.

Had Jason's customers realized that his cakes actually didn't taste very good as well as being far too sweet? Or was the lure of Annie greeting her customers and seating them the reason why their patrons had returned that morning? Whatever it was, Lauren decided not to question it, but to enjoy the brisk business.

Even when they ran out of cupcakes, people still ordered coffee. Lauren smiled at her cousin, who was taking payment for an order.

"Just like old times," she murmured to Zoe.

"Yep!"

***

That afternoon, Lauren relaxed on the sofa, Annie in her lap. She needed to come up with some new cupcake ideas. So far, she and Zoe had come up with a total of … none. Zoe had gone to fetch AJ, the kitten Ed had adopted, for a play date.

Lauren's thoughts drifted. What about maple pecan? Coconut cream? Maple coconut? Coconut pecan? She wrote each flavor down, even if she thought it mightn't work.

Although business had been good that morning, next week Jason might have another trick up his sleeve to tempt their customers back to him.

"We're here!" Zoe's cheery voice roused Lauren from her thoughts.

"Brrt!" Annie jumped off Lauren's lap and trotted to the kitchen.

"Hi, AJ." Lauren greeted the eight-month-old cat. Annie had found the brown tabby Maine Coon when she had been a tiny stray scrap. Ed had instantly fallen in love with her, and taken her home with him.

"Mew!" AJ jumped out of the carrier and greeted Annie. She had a dark brown M in the middle of her forehead and inquisitive eyes.

"Brrt!" Annie led the way into the living room.

"They're so cute." Zoe grinned as she watched the two felines chase a ball around the sofa.

"Definitely." Lauren smiled.

After the playdate was over, Zoe took AJ back to Ed's house.

"Maybe AJ can start training as Annie's assistant at the café," she mused before heading out the door.

"What does Annie think about that?" Lauren was instantly protective of her fur baby. "She's used to being the only cat there."

"We'll have to ask her and see." Zoe grinned, not fazed at all.

"You'll also have to ask AJ and Ed," Lauren pointed out.

"I hadn't thought of that," Zoe admitted. "Hmm."

Zoe left, carefully carrying the cage. AJ mewed goodbye to Annie, who answered in return.

"What do you think of Zoe's idea to have AJ act as your assistant at the café?" Lauren asked Annie as they headed into the living room.

"Brrp." *I'll think about it.*

***

After a pleasant weekend, including her date with Mitch, and brainstorming new flavors with Zoe, Lauren was ready to return to work on Tuesday. She'd noticed Jason's truck on Monday, parked in front of her cottage, but she tried not to let it bother her. There didn't seem to be as many customers at his van once again.

She and Zoe were busy on Monday, anyway, with grocery shopping, testing her new salted caramel cupcake recipe she'd thought up, and visiting Mrs. Finch.

"If he turns up tomorrow," Zoe vowed that evening as they finished eating dinner, "we'll take care of him."

"Yes," Lauren agreed.

"Brrt!"

On Tuesday morning after breakfast, Lauren sat in the living room with Annie.

"I'm going to call Mitch to let him know I'm making his favorite vanilla cupcakes today, as well as salted caramel," Lauren told her. She picked up the cell phone and showed it to the feline.

"Brrt," Annie replied, looking at the device with interest.

"I press this button here." Lauren showed Annie the numbered button that she'd programmed for Mitch.

Annie had already used Lauren's cell phone – she'd called AJ a few months ago, and when Lauren was sick at home with a cold, the feline had worked the video app so they could check in on Zoe taking care of the café.

"Hi, Lauren," Mitch's deep, masculine voice came out of the phone.

"Brrt," Annie said to him.

"Hi, Annie." He sounded surprised to be greeted by her.

"We're both here," Lauren told him, stifling a giggle.

She told him about her cupcake plans for the morning, to which he replied he'd try to stop by later that day to grab a vanilla cupcake, and one of her new salted caramels.

"Brrt," Annie spoke into the phone as Lauren said goodbye to him.

"Bye, Annie." Mitch chuckled, before Lauren ended the call.

"And now we have to go to work." Lauren pocketed her phone and rose from the sofa. So did Annie.

The trio had just opened up the café when the familiar *chug chug, grr grr* filtered through from the street.

"Brrt!" Annie looked annoyed as she sat up in her cat bed.

"I know, Annie," Lauren sympathized.

"I'm calling the town council right now." Zoe dug her phone out of her jeans pocket. "That way, smirky Jason won't know we're reporting him."

"Good idea." Lauren smiled at her.

"I have to leave a message." Zoe tsked.

Ed rattled pastry tins in the kitchen. She was glad he was here – on Saturday people had been disappointed there weren't any of his pastries to choose from, although their regulars knew he didn't work on the weekends.

"Let's hope we get as many customers as we did on Saturday morning." Lauren attempted to be positive.

She looked at her new cupcake creation in the glass case.

The batter was caramel flavored, with made from scratch creamy caramel frosting, and a ribbon of not too sweet caramel sauce swirled around the peaks of the frosting. It was topped off with a small chocolate heart as well as a few sprinkles of high-quality sea salt. She couldn't wait until one of her favorite customers tried it.

"Wait until everyone tries your new salted caramel." Zoe grinned. "I put two away for us for later – and one for Mitch."

"Good thinking." Lauren was proud of her new creation and it was something that she hadn't seen listed at Jason's truck.

Zoe's phone buzzed, and she answered it as Lauren unbolted the entrance door.

"Oh, pooh," she said as she ended the call. "The permit officer is busy at another location right now and can't come and kick Jason off our turf."

"When can he get here?" Lauren frowned as she spied a man grabbing a pink bag from Jason and walking along the sidewalk.

"Maybe this afternoon." Zoe sounded downcast.

"I'm going to see what sort of cupcakes he has today," Lauren told her. "I'll be back in a minute."

"Okay." Zoe sounded distracted.

Lauren told herself she shouldn't go out there to take a look, but she couldn't help herself. It was only to double check that Jason wasn't selling salted caramel cupcakes.

Lauren approached the truck.

"Don't worry, man," she heard Jason, although she couldn't see him at the serving hatch. If it wasn't for his voice, she would have thought that the truck was deserted. "I paid her back last night."

"Good." Another male voice. Was it Jason's friend Scott, who had helped out last week? "She really needs the money, Jase."

"I understand," Jason replied. "But there's no need to worry. We made good money last week with these cupcakes. I told you this was an amazing idea."

"Yeah." Scott didn't sound so convinced. "But you said yourself takings were down the last couple of days."

"If that brat hadn't had a temper tantrum in front of the truck on Saturday, I would have sold out again." Jason sounded angry. "Stupid toddler."

"I'm sure she didn't do it on purpose." Scott sounded surprised at his pal's tone.

"It doesn't matter. I'm sure we'll sell all this stuff today. I can't believe all I have to do is chuck on some shiny silver balls and all the rest and these ladies lap it up." He chuckled.

"I don't think Jessica liked your first batch of cupcakes." Scott said.

"So what? She's not on my radar anymore. And never tell her where I am again, okay? She came down here and made a big scene. Scared off customers."

"I don't know why you had to be so cruel to her," Scott remarked. "What was I supposed to do when she begged me to tell her where you were? You should have seen her, man. It wasn't good."

"Leave Jessica to me. Or not." Jason chuckled. "It's definitely over between us. So forget about her. What we need to concentrate on is buying another van. Then you can drive it and sell these cakes to more ladies."

"What?" Scott sounded shocked. "But you know I'm waiting to hear back about my college application."

"You can go to college anytime," Jason said. "Right now we're making money with these cupcakes. I told you the ladies would go for anything that looks good."

Lauren stepped back from the truck. She thought she'd heard too much to now clear her throat and announce her presence. The dog hadn't barked or growled, so maybe Sweet Boy was having a day off?

She strode back to the café, mulling over what she'd just heard. Jason didn't sound like a nice person, but maybe he had a point about his cupcakes – females had seemed to go wild over them with the huge dollops of frosting and blingy edible decorations – at least, until the last couple of days. Had they finally realized Jason's cupcakes didn't taste as good as they looked?

***

"It will be fun," Zoe enthused to Ed.

Lauren had just returned to the café and found her cousin in the kitchen, chatting to Ed. Mitch had already stopped by and picked up his favorite vanilla, as well as the new salted caramel cupcake – and a kiss from Lauren.

"I don't know," Ed said doubtfully. He looked up in relief as Lauren entered. "What do you think, Lauren?"

"About what?" Lauren was instantly alert. Was it another one of Zoe's wild schemes? Which sometimes worked, she reminded herself.

"I was telling Ed that AJ could come in tomorrow to train as Annie's assistant," Zoe told her.

"Without discussing it with me first?" Lauren asked.

"Oh – sorry. Yeah, I guess we should have talked it over properly first, but I thought what a good opportunity it was to grab Ed while there weren't any customers, and tell him all about it."

"I think Annie is still considering it," Lauren told her.

"And AJ should have a chance to consider it too," he told Zoe. "Maybe she won't like working here. Maybe she only likes playing with Annie."

"But being here at the café is like playing to Annie," Zoe told him. "She has such a good time with the customers, especially her favorites."

"True," Lauren allowed. "But sometimes she likes going home and taking a break, particularly if it's super busy and it becomes a bit overwhelming for her."

"We could try it tomorrow with Annie and AJ," Zoe wheedled. "Please?"

Ed sighed. "I guess it won't do any harm – if AJ wants to do it. She's only eight months old, remember?"

"And Annie has to agree to it," Lauren said quickly.

"I'm sure they'll both want to do it." Zoe brightened. "You'll see!"

***

Later that day, Lauren filled in Zoe on what she'd overheard at the cupcake truck.

"So smirky Jason is an all-around jerk," Zoe commented.

"It seems like it," Lauren agreed.

"I just hope the permit officer comes this afternoon and tells him to get lost."

A customer departed the café, the door open for a moment.

"These cupcakes are no good!" A red-faced man approached the truck parked outside. He brandished a wrinkled pink bag.

"Calm down, man." Jason appeared at the serving hatch.

Lauren and Zoe stared at each other, then hurried over to the door. From their vantage point, they could see and hear everything from the truck.

"Maybe we shouldn't do this," Lauren said doubtfully.

"We totally should!"

"My wife bought me these awful cakes." The angry man shoved the paper bag at Jason.

Sweet Boy growled, his head appearing in the serving hatch, baring his teeth at the disgruntled customer.

So the canine had been there that morning, Lauren thought. Perhaps he'd been napping when she'd overheard Jason and Scott talking inside the truck.

"I told her not to try anything new. That I wanted Lauren's cupcakes." He jerked his thumb at the café. "But she came home raving about your pink truck and the cute dog and how much frosting you put on these – these – things. I thought she was trying to poison me!" He shuddered.

"So you want a refund?" Jason asked.

"Yes, I want a refund!" The man glared at him.

"Do we know him?" Zoe muttered to Lauren.

"No." Lauren shook her head. From the way the man was behaving, she didn't *want* to know him. Maybe he'd never entered the café, and instead his wife bought the cupcakes and brought them home to him. She felt sorry for whoever his wife was, if he was blowing up like this about baked goods. The samples she'd tried of Jason's cakes hadn't been *that* bad, surely? Bad enough to put someone in a rage like this?

"Here." Jason shoved some bills at him. "Don't come back and tell your wife not to, either. Or else I'll call the cops."

"*You'll* call the cops?" The man laughed incredulously. "You've got some nerve, I'll give you that." He stuck the money in his wallet and walked away, shaking his head.

"At least he's not coming in here." Lauren closed the door.

"Good. We don't want customers like that."

"No."

As Lauren turned away from the door, she noticed Jason glowering at her. She bit her lip, sorry that he'd noticed them taking in the scene.

As she went to take payment from a customer, she realized she hadn't seen Jason's friend Scott during that exchange. Had he already taken off? Or had he been a silent observer inside the truck?

CHAPTER 6

The next day, Lauren, Zoe, and Annie entered the café from the private hallway.

"Look!" Zoe pointed to the large window. "Smirky Jason's here already, parked outside our cottage."

"I didn't hear him pull up." Lauren frowned.

"Maybe he came super early. We could have had the microwave on or been in the shower," Zoe suggested.

"That's possible."

"Let's not worry about him," Zoe said.

"Agreed. I'll go and bake the cupcakes." Lauren entered the gleaming commercial kitchen and set to work. Once the cakes were out of the oven, she joined Zoe and Annie in the café area.

"AJ is coming to work with you today, Annie." Zoe grinned.

"Brrt," Annie sounded a little unsure.

"She doesn't have to come and help you if you don't want her to." Lauren bent down to the cat. "Zoe thought you might enjoy having her around, but the decision is up to you." She gave Zoe a pointed stare.

"Of course," Zoe said hastily. "Everyone knows you're in charge of seating the customers, Annie."

"And talking to them," Lauren added. She knew some of their regulars valued their interaction with Annie, especially Annie's favorites, whom she spoke to in a series of brrts and chirps, and appeared to listen to them as they told her about their day.

"Brrp." Annie wandered over to her cat bed and curled up in it.

"Oh, dear." Lauren turned to Zoe. "Perhaps AJ coming in isn't a good idea."

"Perhaps you're right," Zoe replied, doubt flickering over her face. "Maybe we should tell Ed—"

There was a frantic banging on the glass entrance door. Lauren and Zoe turned around. Jessica, Jason's ex, swung her arms wildly in the air.

"He's dead!" she wailed, loud enough for them to hear her through the glass.

"What?" Lauren rushed to unlock the door. "What's wrong?"

"Jason's dead!" Tears streamed down Jessica's face. "And the police are going to think I did it!"

***

Lauren and Zoe raced out of the café.

"Are you sure he's dead?" Lauren tossed over her shoulder as they neared the van. Bits of litter lined the gutters – a tell-tale sign it had been windy the night before. Jessica's red car was parked in front of the pink truck.

"I – I think so," Jessica stumbled after them.

Annie stood in the doorway of the café, watching, her green eyes wide.

"Hello? Jason?" Zoe jumped up on her tiptoes at the serving hatch.

"I can't see anything."

"That's because you have to get inside." Jessica wrenched open the back door of the truck and pointed. "See?"

Jason lay on the floor, a big bloody gash on his head. He wore jeans and a t-shirt, the blood staining some of his blond hair. But for once, he didn't have a smirk on his face.

The coppery scent of blood mixed with Jessica's cloying rose perfume hit Lauren's senses.

Lauren quickly reached for his wrist, trying to find a pulse. There wasn't one. She closed her eyes, hoping she wasn't going to be sick.

"Well?" Zoe asked.

Lauren shook her head, opened her eyes, and gently released Jason's wrist.

She avoided looking at the body and instead focused on the interior of the truck. White cupboards lined each side of the vehicle, apart from where the serving hatch was. A small refrigerator was also included in the layout.

"We have to call the police," Zoe said in a subdued voice, her brown eyes huge.

Lauren dug out her phone from her jeans pocket. And dialed 911. She quickly gave her details.

"Someone will be here as soon as they can," she told them after she ended the call. "We mustn't touch anything."

Jessica's face crumpled, her mascaraed eyes clogged with tears.

"Why don't you come to the café and I'll make you a hot drink?" Zoe placed an arm around her

"I'll guess I'll guard the scene," Lauren said reluctantly. "Make sure Annie stays inside the café."

"Will do." Zoe nodded.

Lauren watched her cousin usher Jessica inside the coffee shop.

What was Jason's ex doing here, anyway? And where was Sweet Boy, and Jason's friend Scott? Although, Scott hadn't seemed to be here every day. Maybe he had another job?

Not that it was any of her business, she told herself.

Mitch. She could call him. Lauren speed dialed him, relief flowing through her as he answered. She quickly told him what had happened, relaxing her grip on the phone a little when he said he'd be there right away.

Lauren paced in front of the truck, careful not to get too close. They'd closed the back door after discovering Jason's body – even though she hadn't liked the guy, she didn't want anyone coming over to gawk at him.

Finally, just when she thought she couldn't stand being out there any longer, a police vehicle pulled up.

After giving her details to the officer, she was allowed to return to the café. She'd just opened the door to go inside when Mitch arrived.

"Are you okay?" Worry creased his face as he strode over to her.

"I'm fine." She allowed herself to nestle in his arms for a moment, then pulled back. "Zoe and I didn't discover the – victim this time. It was his ex-girlfriend Jessica."

"Where is she?"

"Inside." Lauren gestured to the café behind them. "Zoe's looking after her."

"Good." He nodded. "I don't know if I'll be assigned this case. We've finally wrapped up the string of burglaries, but since you're my girlfriend and you're involved …"

"But I'm more of a bystander this time," she protested. "Jessica banged on the café door and told us she'd found Jason in … there." She pointed at the truck, shuddering at the memory of seeing his dead body.

"I'll talk to the officer and tell them to come and see you in the café." Mitch pressed a swift kiss to her forehead.

"Okay." Lauren entered the shop.

"What did Mitch say?" Zoe pounced on her the moment she walked inside. Luckily – or was it? – there weren't any customers, besides Jessica.

"Not much." Lauren sank down on a chair beside Jessica and smiled wanly at her. "How are you holding up?"

"I think I'll be okay." Jessica lifted her tear-streaked face to her. "Zoe's been making sure I have lots of sugar – she gave me a large hot chocolate because she said there aren't any cupcakes ready yet."

"Good." Lauren nodded.

"And now I'm making *you* a big hot chocolate." Zoe started steaming milk. "I had a small one when I made Jessica's, but I think I should have another one as well."

"How's Annie?" Lauren looked over at the cat bed.

"Brrt!" Annie ran over to Lauren and demanded to be cuddled.

Lauren lifted the feline onto her lap and gently stroked her. Annie purred, closing her eyes.

"I wish I had a cat like that," Jessica said.

"You should definitely get one, Jessica," Zoe told her as she brought over the drinks. "Would you like something else?"

"No, I'm good – thanks." Jessica stared through the large windows to the scene outside.

Lauren followed her gaze. Mitch spoke to the uniformed officer, then followed him inside the truck.

"Maybe we shouldn't look," Lauren told her gently.

"Yeah." Jessica grimaced and focused on Annie purring away on Lauren's lap.

"Do you want to talk about it?" Zoe asked, taking a sip of her hot chocolate.

"Not really." Jessica shivered. "It all happened so fast. I couldn't see Jason standing there at the hatch even when I called out. He wasn't in the driver's seat, either. So I went around to the back of the truck and knocked. He didn't answer.

I tried the handle and the door just opened."

"Really?" Zoe exchanged a glance with Lauren.

"Yeah." Jessica nodded. "But who would do such a thing to him? He had it all!"

"Really?" Now it was Lauren's turn.

"I know some people say – said – he was a jerk." Jessica sniffed. "But he was awesome – so good looking, and smart. Even though he had a manual job and wasn't a CEO or something like that. But he could have been if he'd wanted to." She sounded convinced.

"Didn't you say he hurt his hand working construction?" Zoe probed.

"That's right. He complained to the foreman but instead of helping him, they laid him off instead. Said the job was coming to an end anyway and they didn't want complainers. Then he got this idea for the cupcake truck – well, it was really his and Scott's idea."

"Oh?" Lauren asked.

"Yeah. Scott told me he was just joking around one day with Jason and said what a hoot it would be if they made money selling cupcakes. But Jason took the idea seriously, and look!" She pointed to the truck outside. "He even knew to paint the truck pink and put the gold lettering on it. Pink's my favorite color, you know. I told him that once and he must have remembered. That's why I found it hard to believe him when he said it was over between us. Because why would he paint it that color if he didn't want to see me anymore?" She buried her face in her hands.

Lauren and Zoe looked at each other. To get female customers, seemed to be the same thought they had.

The door opened and Mitch strode in, coming over to their table.

"This is Jessica." Lauren gestured to the weeping girl.

"Another detective is going to come out and question you," Mitch told them. "Can you keep Jessica here until then?"

"Sure." Lauren nodded.

"Can I talk to you for a minute?" Mitch asked her, indicating one of the rear tables.

Lauren got up awkwardly, still cradling Annie. She followed him to the back of the room.

"What is it?" she asked.

Annie opened one sleepy eye, saw it was Mitch, and shut it again.

"Is Annie okay?" He frowned at the cat.

"I think so. She's had something else to deal with despite – Jason. I'll tell you about it later."

"Okay. It looks like Jason died immediately – blunt force trauma to the head. But we won't know officially until the medical examiner confirms it."

"What sort of weapon was it?" Lauren asked. She couldn't remember seeing anything obvious.

"Tire wrench. We found it under one of the cupboards."

Lauren shuddered.

"Yeah." He paused. "When the detective questions you, it might get a bit detailed. We don't know why Jason had picked this location for his truck, or why he targeted your café."

"Zoe and I don't know, either." Scenes from last week flashed through Lauren's mind. "What about Scott, Jason's friend? He was with him in the truck yesterday. And Sweet Boy, the dog. We didn't see him there today."

"There was no one else in the truck just now," he told her. "No animals, either."

"Jessica knows Scott," she told him.

"Good." He nodded. "I'll pass that on to the detective who's coming. I wish they'd assigned me, but because of our relationship …"

"I understand," Lauren told him. And she did.

Mitch told her he'd stop by the cottage after work that evening and check she was okay. His phone rang, and he answered it.

"I have to go." He grimaced. "The burglar we arrested only wants to talk to me."

"Go." She shooed him away.

She returned to Zoe and Jessica, Annie still in her arms. Was Annie still out of sorts about AJ coming in for a training session? Or had it been the discovery of Jason's body, even though the feline had only watched from a distance? Or did she know that Lauren needed comforting?

Perhaps it was all three, she mused as she sat down again at the table, nursing the cat.

Zoe had visited the kitchen, informing Ed of the morning's events, then zoomed back to the café area.

"I think maybe we should close for a little while," Zoe told her, after Lauren filled her in on her conversation with Mitch. "If a detective is going to question all three of us – four if we count Ed – we don't want customers getting the wrong idea."

"If we have any," Lauren said gloomily.

"I'll put a sign up on the door." Zoe hurried to the counter, scrawled on a piece of paper, and taped it up on the glass door. "All done."

"I'll have to tell his Mom," Jessica said. "And Scott." She hesitated. "Or will the police do that?"

"I'm sure they will," Lauren told her. "But they'll probably need to get Scott's contact details from you."

"Oh, yeah." Jessica nodded.

A man dressed in a gray suit entered the café and introduced himself as Detective Castern. He accompanied each of them to the rear of the café, including Ed, and took their statements and contact details.

By the time he finished, Lauren needed a latte – or a mocha.

"I guess we can re-open." Zoe pulled down the sign on the door.

"Thanks, guys." Jessica smiled wanly at them. "I'm sorry Jason was trying to take your customers away from you – I also told the detective I was sorry about that."

"You did?" Lauren asked.

"Oh, yeah. He asked me lots of questions about Jason and why he was parked outside. I told him you two make awesome cupcakes and Jason must have found out and that's why he set up his truck here, to sell his cupcakes to your customers."

Zoe looked like she was trying hard not to let steam erupt from the top of her pixie cut.

"Thanks for telling us," Lauren said faintly.

Jessica waved goodbye to them, not seeming to realize that she might have inadvertently caused trouble.

"Brrt?" Annie called from her cat bed. Her usual good mood seemed to have been restored – perhaps it was because the detective had admired her before taking their statements.

"It's okay, Annie," Lauren assured her. "Jessica was being honest, I guess."

"Her honesty could make us look like major suspects." Zoe blew out a breath. "We've got a great big motive for bumping off Jason – he was the reason why business was down."

"But it did seem to bounce back before he was killed," Lauren reminded her. She looked around the empty café. "Until today."

"Yeah, what's up with that?" Zoe drummed her fingertips on the counter. "Where's Hans, and Mrs. Finch, and Ms. Tobin, even?"

"And Martha, Father Mike—"

"Hi!" Brooke, the local hairdresser, entered the café. By her side was Jeff, who owned the flower shop. His previously shaggy sandy hair was now neat and tidy, the look suiting him. He wore a cream button-down shirt tucked neatly into brown slacks, and his blue eyes were framed with square navy metal glasses.

"Hi!" Lauren was genuinely pleased to see the couple. They'd met a few months ago and had seemed instantly smitten with each other.

"What's going on?" Jeff motioned to the bright pink truck outside which still had the uniformed officer guarding it.

Lauren and Zoe filled them in on the events of that morning.

"That's terrible." Brooke looked distressed. "I had no idea that this cupcake guy was even here – I've been swamped with bookings for the last few weeks and my clients have been talking about topics other than cupcakes."

"Like what?" Jeff looked interested.

"Like their boyfriends." Brooke smiled at him fondly. "And then they want to hear all about us."

"So that's why you haven't been in here lately," Zoe said.

Brooke nodded. "I've also had some more requests for home visits – Mrs.

Finch told her friends that I come to her house to cut her hair, so that's taken up some of my time as well. But it's worth it."

Annie showed the couple to a table, and sat with them for a while. Lauren and Zoe whipped up the order of two large lattes and two salted caramel cupcakes.

"Hot chocolate, stat!" Martha barreled in, pushing her walker.

"Brrt!" Annie scampered to greet her friend, hopping onto the padded seat of the walker without waiting to be invited.

"We're definitely friends again." Martha beamed at Annie. "Let's go, cutie pie." She pushed the walker, Annie's paws pressed securely on the padded seat as they wheeled through the café, stopping at a table when Annie issued a commanding, "Brrt."

A wave of seniors followed Martha into the café.

Lauren's eyes widened at the unexpected business.

"We had a huge craft club morning at the senior center," Martha called to them from her table in the middle of the room.

"Now everyone's dying for coffee and cupcakes."

"What's going on out there?" A plump woman asked them, pointing to the police presence at the pink truck outside.

Lauren and Zoe glanced at each other. What should they say?

"Don't tell me someone's been murdered," Martha joked. She sobered when Lauren and Zoe didn't answer. "They haven't, have they? And I just said we're dying for cupcakes!"

"Yes," Lauren and Zoe blurted.

"Brrt."

There was a lot of tsking among the crowd, with everyone asking the duo for details.

Lauren and Zoe told them briefly who the victim was.

"I never liked his cupcakes," one man said.

"Far too sweet," a woman said. "I thought they were going to rot my dentures!"

"I'm sorry I ever tried those cupcakes," another woman said. She looked embarrassedly at Lauren and Zoe.

"I felt like a traitor. That's why I haven't been in again – until now."

"Everyone's welcome here," Lauren told them.

"That's right." Zoe nodded. "Even if you did buy his cakes."

"Zoe!" Lauren hissed.

They took everyone's orders and set to work, making lattes, mochas, hot chocolates, and a few pots of tea.

"We're going to be sold out at this rate." Zoe picked up the last salted caramel cupcake with shiny silver tongs and placed it on a plate. "And Ed's pastries have nearly all gone as well."

"Good." Lauren couldn't wait to count the day's takings. She hadn't liked to tell Zoe she'd been worried about business being down so much. Hopefully everything was back to normal now.

After a busy couple of hours, they finally had time for a break.

"Brrt!" Annie pounced on something near the rear of the café.

"What's that, Annie?" Lauren headed over to her.

"Brrt." Annie patted the small scrap of … paper?

"Can I see it?" Lauren asked her.

"Brrp." Annie pushed the fragment over to her with her paw.

Lauren picked it up and turned it over.

"What is it?" Zoe hurried over to them.

"It might be part of a photo." Lauren frowned.

"You think?" Zoe peered at the glossy scrap about an inch in size. "Yeah, it could be."

"It's pink," Lauren said.

"Isn't that Jessica's favorite color?" Zoe said. "Maybe she dropped it when she was in here earlier."

"Or maybe she walked it in and it has nothing to do with her," Lauren countered.

"Yep, it was super windy last night," Zoe commented. "Did you see all the litter out there when we went to check on Jason's dead – you know."

"I know." Lauren shivered at the hours old memory.

"Maybe I walked it in," Zoe suggested. "Or you."

"True," Lauren agreed.

"Or one of our customers. Huh."

"What should we do with it?"

"I know, I'll put it in my ashtray where we've put our keys," Zoe proposed. "Just in case. It's Annie's Lost and Found again."

"Brrt!"

Zoe zipped to the cottage and was back in less than two minutes. "Safe and sound in my ashtray." She grinned.

"Good." Lauren nodded. "Do you think we should cancel AJ's training session this afternoon?"

"But we've been interviewed," Zoe replied. "And we've already told Annie it's happening. Ed's probably told AJ as well. We don't want to disappoint them, do we?"

"Or do you mean *you* don't want to be disappointed?" Lauren asked. "I'm not sure if Annie is as sold on the idea as you are."

"But we can give it a try, can't we?" Zoe pleaded. "I think it will be so cute! And maybe Annie would like to share her duties with AJ."

"Well, if it's okay with Annie," Lauren said dubiously. At least the café wasn't busy at the moment.

"I'll tell Ed." Zoe raced to the kitchen before Lauren could change her mind.

"Ed's gone home to fetch AJ," Zoe announced barely two minutes later. "He says all afternoon might be too much for her, but we could give it a try for an hour or so."

"Okay,' Lauren replied, thinking that Ed probably felt the same way she did about the whole notion – dubious.

A little while later, Ed clomped into the café from the front door, carrying AJ's cage.

"I don't know about this." He set the carrier down on the floor.

"Brrt!" Annie trotted over to greet her friend.

"Mew!" AJ poked one paw out of the metal squares, her eyes shining brightly.

"Annie, would you like to show AJ how to help you this afternoon?" Lauren asked.

"You could show her how to seat customers at tables," Zoe added.

"Brrp." Annie seemed to be mulling it over.

"You don't have to, Annie," Ed told her. "Maybe I should just take AJ home again."

"Mew!" AJ sounded cross.

"I think AJ wants to stay here with Annie." Zoe giggled.

"I guess we could try it," Lauren said. "But we'll have to make sure the front door is shut at all times. We don't want AJ getting out on the street." She knew Annie had enough sense to stay inside the café – apart from the couple of times lately with the drama from Jason's truck.

"Definitely," Ed said. "AJ's microchipped, but I wouldn't want anything happening to her."

"I understand." Lauren nodded.

"Let's do this!" Zoe opened up the carrier.

"Meow!" AJ jumped out and greeted Annie.

"Brrt." Annie led the way to her basket, glancing at AJ over her shoulder, as if encouraging the younger cat to follow her.

They watched as Annie indicated to AJ that she could share her basket with her. The two of them cuddled up together, but

Annie's expression was alert as she took in the few occupied tables.

Ms. Tobin stepped into the café.

"Brrt." Annie hopped out of the basket and trotted over to greet her.

AJ stayed in the basket, her eyes wide. Then she jumped out and ran to Ed. "Mew!"

"Go with Annie," he told the cat. "Watch what she does."

AJ emitted a low grumble and joined Annie at the *Please Wait to be Seated* sign.

"I'm sure AJ will be okay," Zoe told him.

"All right. I'll clean up the kitchen before I leave." Ed clomped into the kitchen, closing the swinging door behind him. AJ ran after him. "Meow!" She was too late – the door shut her out.

"You're not allowed in there, AJ." Lauren joined the cat. "Only humans are allowed in the kitchen. But you can stay out here with Annie – and us."

"Meow!" AJ rapidly blinked, as if trying not to cry. "Meow!"

"Goodness, Lauren, what is going on here?" Ms. Tobin called.

"Annie is training her assistant," Zoe told her brightly.

"It doesn't seem to be going too well," Ms. Tobin tutted as she followed Annie to a small table near the counter. "You might have to put a lot of time into training this cat, Annie."

"Brrt."

"It's AJ." Zoe came over to Ms. Tobin and Annie. "Do you remember her? Annie found her in the garden and Ed adopted her."

"Oh, yes." Ms. Tobin's expression cleared. "The poor little thing. I'm sure you'll be very kind and patient with her, Annie, and show her what to do."

"Brrt." *I'll try.*

"Mew!" AJ scratched at the kitchen door.

"What's wrong?" Ed stuck his head out, then looked down. "AJ, you're not allowed in here." His tone was gentle.

"That's what I told her," Lauren said. "But I think she wants you."

"I wondered if this would be too much for her." Ed frowned. "Maybe she just wants to play. She's not like this when she has a play date with Annie, is she?"

"No," Lauren replied. "The two get along like best friends."

"AJ, come and see what Annie is doing," Zoe called out to her.

With a sigh, AJ wandered over to Annie, sitting at Ms. Tobin's table. Ed went back inside the kitchen.

"Brrt." Annie hopped off the chair, seeming to encourage her friend to jump onto it.

"Hello, dear." Ms. Tobin smiled at AJ. "Would you like to sit with me for a little bit?"

"Brrp." Annie nudged AJ, indicating the chair in front of them.

"Mew!" AJ ran back to the kitchen door. "Meow!" She scratched frantically at the door.

"Maybe she just needs time to become assimilated," Zoe mused.

"Maybe she just needs to go home." Lauren knocked on the kitchen door. "Ed, AJ wants you."

The door opened immediately. Ed bent down and picked up the bundle of brown fur.

"What's wrong?" He scratched AJ behind the ear. The Maine Coon purred instantly and snuggled into his arms.

"I don't think this is going to work out," Lauren said, her eyes a little misty at the sight of the big, gruff man being so gentle with the feline.

"Yeah." Ed nodded.

"Why don't you take her home and have the rest of the afternoon off?" Lauren proposed. "Zoe and I can finish cleaning the kitchen."

"If you're sure." He stepped into the café and grabbed the carrier.

"Is AJ going home already?" Zoe sounded disappointed.

"I don't think AJ's ready to do this." Ed sounded certain. "She's not even one year old. But she can still have play dates with Annie, if Annie wants to." He glanced over at Annie.

"Brrt." *Yes.*

CHAPTER 7

That evening, Mitch stopped by the cottage after dinner. Zoe discreetly left the two of them alone in the living room, saying she was going to text Chris.

"So what was up with Annie today?" Mitch asked as he sat beside Lauren on the couch. He looked over at Annie, sitting in the armchair, her expression alert, as if she knew he was talking about her.

Lauren told him about Zoe's idea to train AJ as Annie's assistant, and AJ's antics that afternoon. Mitch chuckled. "It looks like you've got the café to yourself, Annie."

"Brrt." *Yes.*

"If you'd told me a year ago that I'd be talking to a cat like a regular person, I would have thought they were crazy," he admitted to Lauren.

"But you're not." She smiled softly at him. When she'd met him, he'd told her he'd never had a cat, or had much to do with them. Annie seemed to have gradually changed his attitude, though.

They spent a pleasant evening together watching a TV show, Lauren snuggled in his arms, Annie sitting on the other side of Lauren. When it was time for him to leave, he kissed her goodnight.

"Be careful if the detective talks to you again about Jason's death," he cautioned. "I heard at the station today that he considers you and Zoe major suspects."

***

"Eeek!" Zoe's pixie cut seemed to stand on end as Lauren told her the news. She'd just put her PJs on, and now stood in front of Lauren and Annie in a red t-shirt with matching red cotton sleep shorts.

"I know." Lauren nodded, trying not to be shaken by the news. At least Mitch hadn't told her that before they watched TV. She wouldn't have been able to concentrate, or enjoy spending time with him.

"Brrt!"

"What are we going to do about it?" Zoe demanded.

"Apart from saying we're innocent, what can we do?"

"Investigate!"

"Brrt!" *Investigate!*

"First, we need to make a suspect list." Zoe looked around, as if expecting a piece of paper or a device to suddenly materialize. "Where's my phone?"

"I haven't seen it," Lauren replied.

"We'll have to grab a piece of paper from somewhere. And a pen."

"There's scrap paper in the kitchen."

Zoe and Annie rushed to the kitchen, Lauren following.

"Should we do this now?" She stifled a yawn as she sat down at the kitchen table. "We've got to get up early tomorrow and open the café."

"I know, but this is important."

"Brrt!"

"Jessica." Zoe scratched on the piece of paper.

"You think Jessica killed Jason?" Lauren sounded shocked.

"I don't know," Zoe admitted. "But she was there at the scene, wasn't she?

And you know what they say – there's a good chance that the person who discovers the body is the killer!"

"Who says that?"

"Everyone." Zoe waved a hand in the air, as if citing her sources wasn't important. She tapped the pen on the kitchen table. "And his friend Scott."

"Why would Scott kill Jason?"

"I don't know." Zoe looked exasperated. "You're not playing along, Lauren."

"Sorry." Lauren covered her mouth in an attempt to halt another yawn. "It's late and I just want to go to bed."

"Ooh, I know!" Zoe scribbled something. "The angry man who demanded a refund on the cupcakes."

"That's right." Lauren sat up a little straighter.

"He was very upset about the cupcakes not tasting good, wasn't he?"

"Brrt," Annie agreed.

"So that's three suspects," Lauren said.

"And us. Zoe and Lauren." Zoe scratched down their names.

"You're putting *us* on the suspect list?" Lauren's eyes widened.

"I know *we* didn't do it," Zoe told her, "but that detective seems to think so, if what Mitch told you was true."

"That's a depressing thought."

"It certainly is." Zoe sounded far too cheerful. But Lauren reminded herself that her cousin enjoyed investigating the murders that sometimes occurred in the small town, dragging her reluctantly along.

"Anyone else?' Lauren asked.

"Not that I can think of right now," Zoe admitted.

"Then maybe we should go to bed." Lauren rose.

"Good night, Mom." Zoe giggled, then patted Lauren's arm. "We can think up more suspects tomorrow."

***

They didn't get a chance to talk further about the murder until late the next morning. They were busy with customers from the time they opened until eleven o'clock.

Ed informed them that AJ had been fine once he'd taken her home, but he didn't think becoming Annie's assistant was a good idea for the Maine Coon, and they both agreed, Zoe reluctantly.

Finally, they were able to sit down on the stools behind the counter and grab a mocha each.

"I definitely need this." Zoe sighed as she sipped on the cocoa-laced coffee. Ms. Tobin was the only customer right now, and she was talking to Annie at a table in the middle of the room.

"Ooh, Ms. Tobin!" Zoe jumped up, stuck her hand in her jeans pocket, and pulled out a piece of paper.

"Don't tell me that's last night's suspect list," Lauren said, keeping her voice low.

"Yep." Zoe grinned.

"And you think Ms. Tobin is a suspect?" Lauren glanced over at the middle-aged woman.

"Well, not really," Zoe admitted. "But she did say she didn't care for Jason's cupcakes. And about never trusting a smirking man."

Lauren watched her write down Ms. Tobin's name.

"I think you should put that list away," she murmured. "We don't want to give anyone the wrong impression – including Ms. Tobin."

"I guess." Zoe reluctantly tucked the piece of paper back into her pocket. "There. Out of sight."

They finished their mochas, Lauren wondering if they would have a lunch rush today, or if the rest of the day would be quiet. She was just about to ask Zoe if she wanted to take her break first, when Scott walked into the café, wearing jeans and a t-shirt, looking a little unsure as to his welcome.

"It's Smirky Jason's friend!" Zoe dug her elbow into Lauren's ribcage.

"I can see that," Lauren muttered. She rose from the stool. "Hi."

Annie jumped down from the chair at Ms. Tobin's table and trotted over to him. "Brrt?"

"You're a nice cat." Scott smiled down at her.

"Brrp."

"Annie will show you to a table," Lauren told him.

"Really?" He looked like he didn't quite believe her. "Okay."

Annie led the way to a four-seater at the rear. "Brrt."

"I'm going to take his order," Zoe whispered to Lauren. "I wonder what he's doing here."

"I'll come with you."

"What can we get you?" Zoe whipped out her order pad as they approached Scott. Annie sat in the chair opposite him, looking at him inquiringly.

"Um – well – I really wanted to come in and apologize to you guys." Scott looked uncomfortable. "What Jason did wasn't cool – trying to steal your customers like that."

"Thanks," Lauren replied. "We appreciate that."

"Yeah," Zoe replied. "So why did he target us?"

Scott squirmed in his seat. "He told me that a lady friend of his raved about your cupcakes, and your coffee, and he thought it would be easy to set up the truck outside. He didn't think there'd be any problems with permits or law enforcement, because this is a small town."

"Well, he got that right," Zoe muttered.

Lauren silently agreed. Even Mitch warning off Jason hadn't done the trick for long.

"I wanted to let you know I won't be continuing with the truck. I've been accepted into college." His expression brightened. "I'm going to study earth sciences and get into environmental consulting."

"What's that?" Zoe asked.

"It's how I can have an impact on future generations," he told them earnestly. "I can advise developers how to tread more lightly on the earth – instead of ramming in big housing projects that don't leave any room for lawns or trees or wildlife, I can show them how much better it would be for the environment if certain species of trees were planted in a particular area, and which bushes and flowers to choose to help the native wildlife. Like planting the right kind of flowering bushes so that butterflies and bees can flourish, even in suburbia or the city."

"That sounds cool," Lauren remarked.

"It is." He nodded. "Did you know that the world's population of bees is dying off? They need as much help as we can give them, or one day there won't be any bees to pollinate our food."

"That's a scary thought." Zoe grimaced.

Scott ordered a large latte and a lavender cupcake.

"Won't be long," Lauren promised, as she and Zoe headed back to the counter.

"He seems much nicer than Jason," Zoe said as she plated the cupcake.

"I know," Lauren said, as she steamed milk for the coffee.

"I wonder why he was hanging out with Jason?" Zoe pondered.

"Didn't Jessica say they were childhood friends?"

"Oh, yeah." Zoe snapped her fingers. "That's right. Hmm. Maybe I should cross him off my suspect list."

"Because he's too nice to be a killer?" Lauren teased.

"That's right." Zoe grinned.

They brought the order over to him, Annie still keeping him company.

"I didn't see Sweet Boy yesterday," Zoe remarked as she set the cupcake down in front of him.

"Who?" Scott looked bewildered.

"The French bulldog," Lauren explained. "I think Jason said his real name was Butch?"

"Oh." Scott's face cleared. "Yeah. Butch belongs to Jason's grandfather, and he wanted Butch with him yesterday. He said he had plans to go to the park, and that Butch gets the ladies for him." He glanced at them. "Sorry."

"No worries," Zoe told him. "I'm afraid I didn't think Sweet Boy/Butch was very cute, unlike some of the ladies who bought cupcakes from Jason."

"I know, right?" Scott grimaced. "In fact, this whole cupcake truck idea started off as a joke. It was my idea and then Jason said we could totally do it and he even knew where we could sell the cakes."

"Where did you get the truck from?" Lauren asked.

"Jason bought it. See, me and Jason—" he looked proud and embarrassed at the same time "—won the lottery."

"No way!" Zoe gasped, her brown eyes huge.

"Not the first prize," Scott hastened to assure her. "Thirty-k. So we had enough to buy this secondhand truck. Jason insisted it would be a huge moneymaker and we'd split the profits."

"Did he bake the cupcakes himself?" Lauren asked, her professional interest piqued.

"Yeah." Scott nodded. "But he didn't bake them from scratch. He used box mixes."

"I knew it," Lauren murmured under her breath.

"And he bought the frosting as well," Scott continued. "The cheapest he could find. He even started clipping coupons to get the best deals he could."

"Huh," Zoe muttered.

"He said he didn't care what the cupcakes tasted like, he thought the ladies would go ga-ga over them because of the huge amount of frosting he put on them, and all the decorations."

"I think he was right," Lauren replied. "At first, anyway."

"Yeah, he complained about business being down the last couple of days." Scott paused, as if remembering that his friend was no longer here.

"That's when some of our customers returned to us," Zoe remarked.

"So what will you do with the van now?" Lauren asked.

"Sell it, I suppose." Scott shrugged. "I don't know if anyone will want to buy it as is, though. Jason had it painted that bright pink, and did the gold lettering himself."

"It looks like it," Zoe muttered.

Lauren nudged her cousin in a warning manner.

"We're sorry for your loss," Lauren said, realizing that should have been the first thing she'd said to him.

"Thanks." He nodded.

"How's Jessica holding up?" Zoe asked.

"Not good. I don't know what she saw in Jason – yeah, he was good looking, and my friend, but he was a real ladies' man, you know? He liked to play the field."

"Even when he was dating Jessica?" Lauren asked.

Scott hesitated. "Yeah," he finally said.

"And she still wanted him back?" Zoe probed.

"Uh-huh. Even when she found out he'd cheated on her." He shrugged, as if he couldn't understand that.

They left him alone to enjoy his treats.

"I hope his coffee isn't too cold by now," Lauren said.

"We were talking to him for a while," Zoe said in satisfaction, "and got some good info, too."

"But not another viable suspect to look at," Lauren commented.

"Nope."

CHAPTER 8

Mrs. Finch came in that afternoon and they filled her in on Jason's death.

"My goodness," she exclaimed. "Whoever would have thought that would happen?"

They showed her Zoe's suspect list.

"We must talk more about this tomorrow night at craft club," she said. "How is your pottery coming along, Zoe?"

Guilt flashed across Zoe's face. "I haven't done any this week, Mrs. Finch. Not with everything that's happened."

"That's understandable." Mrs. Finch nodded. "What about you, Lauren? Have you decided on your next knitting project?"

Now it was Lauren's turn to look just as uncomfortable as her cousin. "No," she murmured.

"You might come up with some ideas tomorrow night." Mrs. Finch smiled.

***

On Friday evening, the three of them arrived at Mrs. Finch's house.

"Come in, come in." The elderly lady beamed at them, her face wreathed in smiles.

"Brrt!" Annie greeted her.

"Hello, Annie, dear. You'll have to tell me what you've been up to today."

"Brrt." *I will.*

They walked down the lilac painted hall to the living room, decorated in tones of fawn and beige.

"Well now," Mrs. Finch began as she sat down in an armchair, "have you made any progress with your suspect list?"

Lauren and Zoe glanced at each other.

"No," they replied at the same time.

"That is a shame," Mrs. Finch said sympathetically.

"Who do you think the killer is?" Zoe asked her.

"Brrt!" Annie perched on the arm of Mrs. Finch's chair.

"Let me see." Mrs. Finch stroked Annie and closed her eyes. "Tell me more about the angry man who complained about the cupcakes."

Lauren and Zoe told her what they remembered.

"Why, that sounds like Betty's husband." Mrs. Finch opened her eyes. "She's always said he loves cakes and cookies, and gets upset if there aren't any in the house when he wants a treat."

"He doesn't sound very nice," Zoe remarked.

"Oh, he can be quite charming when he puts his mind to it." Mrs. Finch laughed. "He works very hard, and he doesn't drink. I suppose eating sweet things is his way of unwinding."

"I hope we don't become like him one day." Zoe eyed Lauren.

"Me neither." Lauren thought guiltily of the cupcake she'd enjoyed for dessert that evening. Had she been eating too many of them? She hadn't kept up with her promise to herself to become fitter during the last few months, either. But she and Zoe didn't get angry if they'd sold out of cupcakes for the day and there weren't any left over to take home for themselves. Did they?

"I'll call Betty tomorrow and have a nice chat with her, and tell her I heard about an altercation at the cupcake truck. I'm sure she'll tell me if her husband was involved," Mrs. Finch offered.

"Would you?" Zoe sounded delighted.

"As long as it doesn't put you in any danger," Lauren added. Was it a good idea to involve Mrs. Finch like this?

"I'm sure it won't."

The conversation soon turned to Zoe's current hobby.

"I'm not sure what to make next in pottery class," Zoe admitted.

"You're not getting bored with it, are you?" Lauren teased.

"No." Zoe's brunette pixie locks swung vehemently as she shook her head. "I'm looking forward to using the wheel more. But the instructor said first we need to familiarize ourselves with the clay which is why I had to make those ashtrays." She sighed. "I hope I'm better at making vases or plates or bowls – or mugs! Yeah, mugs! I could make some for the café!" She turned shining brown eyes to Lauren.

"Good idea." Lauren wanted to be supportive.

"Don't worry," Zoe reassured her, "I hereby give you permission to refuse any of my mugs or anything else from my pottery efforts unless they're good."

"We could even paint the name of the café on the mugs – ooh! – we could paint a picture of Annie on the mugs as well!"

"Brrt!" Annie's ears pricked and she looked pleased at the suggestion.

"You mean you'll be doing all this painting," Lauren said. "I'm not good at that sort of thing."

"Yes, that's what I meant," Zoe agreed quickly.

"It sounds a marvelous idea, Zoe," Mrs. Finch commented. "I'm sure you'll be able to do it if you put your mind to it."

"Exactly," Zoe said with enthusiasm.

Lauren and Zoe made coffee using Mrs. Finch's pod machine, then they said goodnight.

"I can't wait until my next pottery class," Zoe said as they left the cottage. "Wait until I tell the instructor what I have in mind!"

"I can't wait until we hear back from Mrs. Finch's investigation," Lauren said.

"I just hope we haven't put her in any danger."

"What harm could it do for her to call a friend and talk about the cupcake truck? I'm sure Mrs. Finch will be fine."

CHAPTER 9

Lauren and Zoe visited Mrs. Finch on Sunday, after church. They hadn't been for a while, and Lauren's conscience insisted they attend that morning.

She'd worried about Mrs. Finch calling her friend, no matter what Zoe had said.

"I'm fine, dears," Mrs. Finch told them as she opened the door. "I was just about to call you and let you know what happened."

"What did happen?" Zoe asked eagerly.

"Brrt?" Annie wanted to know too.

Once they were settled in the living room, Mrs. Finch filled them in.

"I was right – that man was Betty's husband." Mrs. Finch looked delighted with her sleuthing efforts. "We had a lovely talk on the phone, and Betty is coming to visit me tomorrow afternoon. It's been a while since we've seen each other."

"That's great!" Zoe grinned.

"Someone else had already told her about the altercation – they must have been across the street when her husband lost her temper with that young cupcake man. Anyway, her husband was very remorseful about his behavior and promised it wouldn't happen again."

"Does he have an alibi for around the time of the murder?" Lauren asked.

"It must have occurred sometime in the morning," Zoe mused. "Before we opened at nine-thirty."

"The cupcake truck wasn't there when we closed the day before."

"And I glanced out of the front window that night," Zoe said. "I didn't see the truck lurking outside then." She glanced at Lauren. "Sorry, I meant to tell you that before now.""

Lauren nodded.

"Betty says he was with her that morning," Mrs. Finch informed them. "She said he surprised her by making breakfast for both of them – chocolate chip pancakes – and had arranged to go into the office a little later."

"Hmm." Zoe tapped her cheek. "I wonder if he did that because he was worried someone would report his bad behavior to his wife, so he decided to make amends first? That way, when she found out about him making a scene at the cupcake truck, she couldn't be so mad at him."

"Zoe!" Sometimes Lauren was surprised at how her cousin's mind worked – although she should be used to it by now.

"I must admit I thought along the same lines." Mrs. Finch looked a little uncomfortable. "But that means, surely, that Betty's husband isn't the killer?"

"It seems like it," Lauren agreed.

"Have the police interviewed him?" Zoe asked.

"Yes." Mrs. Finch nodded. "Somehow they found out that he'd been irate about the cupcakes and had confronted the cupcake man – Jason."

"It wasn't us," Lauren said.

"No." Zoe shook her head.

"I'm sure it wasn't." Mrs. Finch smiled at them. "But I would understand if it had been. The police need to have all the facts so they can solve the case."

"Definitely," Lauren agreed.

"But sometimes *we* solve the case instead," Zoe said with relish.

"Hopefully this time, the police can do it," Lauren replied.

Zoe mumbled something under her breath. Lauren didn't want to know what it was.

They enjoyed a cup of coffee while Annie lapped delicately from a bowl of water. Then they said goodbye to Mrs. Finch and walked home.

***

To Lauren's delight, Mitch stopped by the house that afternoon. He'd had to work an extra shift yesterday, so they hadn't seen each other last night.

"I want you to be prepared for this coming week," he told her. Zoe had gone outside to enjoy the April sun. Annie had stayed behind and was now perched on the back of the sofa, looking at them inquisitively.

"Why? What's wrong?" Lauren crinkled her brow.

"The detective in charge of the case says he's determined to solve it quickly. So he might re-interview you and Zoe."

"Okay." Lauren nodded. "What about Jessica, Jason's ex-girlfriend? And Scott, his friend? Is he going to re-interview them?"

"I'm sure he'll be talking to them as well," Mitch replied, his expression serious. "But he seems to be interested in you and Zoe – being right on the scene, and losing business because of the cupcake truck."

"But Jessica was right on the scene, too!" Lauren was indignant. "She found Jason – not me or Zoe."

"I know," he soothed her. "But he can't find any evidence that Jessica was there earlier to kill Jason – unless she drove a totally different car so no one would realize she was in town. Then she could have murdered Jason, left the scene, then return later driving her red car and pretended to find the vic – Jason."

"Is he looking into that theory?" Lauren asked.

"I hope so." Mitch grimaced. "I've already spoken to him about the case, and vouched for you and Zoe, but he says of course I would say my girlfriend is innocent."

"If he questions me again, I'll definitely tell him we're innocent," Lauren said determinedly.

"He also thinks it's convenient that Jason was killed right outside your cottage. It would be easy for you or Zoe to slip out in the early morning and kill him, without anyone seeing."

"But why would Jason be out there at that time?" Lauren frowned. "Are you talking about four or five a.m., something like that?"

"Yes. It's possible." Mitch nodded. "I know it doesn't make much sense that Jason would arrive so early, but we don't even know when he showed up in Gold Leaf Valley that morning. We've only got an approximate time of death from the autopsy. It could have been later, like seven or eight o'clock. What time did you notice his truck there that morning?"

"Around eight. I did think it was a bit strange," Lauren mused. "Jason usually showed up around nine-thirty, when we were already in the café. But that day, we saw his van when we started to get the café ready."

"Maybe he thought he'd grab some customers before you opened," Mitch suggested. "Especially since you told me business had been down for him the last couple of days."

They spoke about more pleasant topics for a while, then Mitch suggested they get something to eat from Gary's Burger Diner.

"That sounds great." Lauren smiled. "Let me check if Zoe wants me to bring something back for her."

Zoe put in an order for a smoky barbecue special and fries. "It's a shame Chris isn't here, otherwise we could double date!"

"That's certainly an idea." Mitch sounded a little dubious.

"I think it could be fun," Lauren said. Maybe it would be.

"Why don't you leave it to me and Lauren?" Zoe proposed. "We'll handle the details."

"Okay," Mitch hesitated. "As long as Chris agrees."

"I'm sure he will." Zoe grinned.

Lauren enjoyed her early dinner with Mitch. The weather was sunny with a cool breeze that gently ruffled her shoulder-length hair as they left the diner and walked back to the cottage, carrying Zoe's take-out order, and a plain burger patty for Annie.

"Brrt!" Annie ran to greet them when they stepped inside the cottage.

"Yes, it's for you." Lauren smiled at the cat. The tantalizing aroma of the beef had been hard to ignore on the stroll home, although she'd already enjoyed her burger at the diner.

She broke up the patty for Annie and placed it in her dish in the kitchen.

"Brrp." Annie sniffed at the meat, then her pink tongue darted out, tasting the meat. Soon the bowl was empty.

"Yum, smoky barbecue!" Zoe dived into her burger and fries.

"Would you like some coffee?" Lauren asked Mitch.

"Thanks, but I've got an early start tomorrow. I'd better head home."

Lauren walked him out to the porch.

"Good night," she said softly.

"Good night." He kissed her tenderly. "Let me know how it goes with the detective if he re-interviews you."

"I will." She touched her gold L letter necklace.

Lauren waved goodbye to him as she watched him get into his car and start the engine. Zoe came up behind her.

"I've spoken to Chris and he thinks a double-date will work. Now all we have to do is find a time that will suit all four of us!"

***

The next day, Lauren and Zoe talked about their plans for the upcoming double date.

"What are we going to do on this date?" Lauren asked as they left for the grocery store.

"Bowling." Zoe grinned. "Or ice skating. Or mini-golf."

"I didn't know you skated," Lauren said.

"I don't. But I think it could be fun."

"And I think we could fall over a bunch of times." Lauren remembered the one time she'd tried ice skating – and the number of times she'd fallen over. It wasn't something she wished to repeat.

"Then Chris could help me up." Zoe's eyes sparkled. "And Mitch could help you up."

"True." Lauren couldn't help smiling at her cousin's enthusiasm.

"Ooh, I know! We could go to a farmers' market in Sacramento!"

"I like that idea." Lauren's eyes lit up.

"Okay, so that's what we'll do." Zoe pulled out her phone and started texting. "Chris," she explained as Lauren parked in front of the small grocery store. "What about next weekend?" She turned to Lauren.

"Works for me," Lauren replied. "I'll have to check with Mitch."

"You could text him right now." Zoe was on a roll.

Lauren preferred talking to texting, but she followed her cousin's advice and sent a brief message to Mitch.

A few seconds later, her phone buzzed.

"Mitch says it's fine with him."

"Good. And it's okay with Chris – he said he can meet us there, since he lives in Sacramento, and he'll send us the details." Zoe high-fived Lauren.

They did their grocery shopping, Lauren planning the cupcake menu for the next week.

She would definitely make more salted caramel cupcakes, as well as lavender, and white chocolate cherry.

"Hans!" Lauren stopped the cart before she barged into the dapper gentleman standing in the next aisle.

"Hello, Lauren and Zoe," Hans replied.

"We haven't seen you in the café lately," Zoe said. "Are you okay?"

"Ach, yes. Just a little cold this last week. But I am better now." He smiled. "I'm sure I will be at the café tomorrow."

"Good," Lauren replied. "I know Annie missed you this last week."

"And I her." He indicated his cart containing fruit and a few cans of soup. "I'm just picking up some things."

"So are we." Zoe grinned.

After a few minutes of small talk, they said goodbye to Hans and continued with their shopping.

"Annie will be glad when he comes in tomorrow," Lauren mused.

"Ooh, we must update him on the murder."

"I wonder if he heard about the altercation between Betty's angry husband and Jason – before Jason died," Lauren remarked.

"We'll have to ask him tomorrow!"

CHAPTER 10

The next morning, Hans came in shortly after they opened the café.

"Brrt!" Annie ran to greet him.

"Hello, *Liebchen.*" Hans bent stiffly to stroke the silver-gray tabby.

"Brrt." *This way.* Annie slowly led him to a four-seater near the counter.

Hans sank down into the pine chair. Annie hopped up on the opposite one.

"What can we get you?" Lauren headed toward them, Zoe by her side. They didn't provide table service as a rule, unless the customer was elderly, infirm, or harried. But Hans was one of their special customers, and besides, they wanted to catch him up on what had happened last week.

Zoe launched into the news about Jason's murder.

"But that is horrible." Hans paled. "What he did, to set up shop outside the café was not nice, but I do not think he should have died."

"That's true." Lauren nodded.

"We didn't do it," Zoe protested.

"Of course not." Hans smiled gently at them. "It was just a shock to hear such a thing."

They informed him about the angry man complaining about his cupcakes to Jason and making a scene.

"*Ja*, I know who this might be." Hans nodded. "It is Betty's husband. He certainly likes his sweets." He patted his slight paunch. "I must be careful I do not get carried away with sugar, but your cupcakes, Lauren, and Ed's pastries, are hard to resist."

"Don't I know it," Lauren said ruefully, thinking of the Danishes and cupcakes she'd enjoyed last week.

They took his order of a cappuccino and an apricot Danish.

As Lauren dusted the chocolate powder on top of the microfoam, she paused. "Do you think we should change to a darker chocolate for our beverages?" she asked Zoe. "Lately, a few people have been mentioning the dangers of too much sugar."

She prided herself on ordering the best quality ingredients she could find, and the hot chocolate powder was no exception. It consisted of fifty percent cocoa, whereas she knew many other cafes used a weaker ratio, such as thirty percent or less of cocoa, the rest of the volume made up of sugar and milk solids.

Zoe gave her a shocked gaze. "But I love this chocolate powder!"

"I do, too," Lauren replied. "But what if we could find a darker one, such as sixty or even seventy percent cocoa?"

"What if we gave customers a choice?" Zoe proposed. "This one, or the new one?"

"Good idea." Lauren smiled. "After work, I'll see if I can find one online."

"Or we could make our own!"

Lauren's eyes widened. Why hadn't she thought of that? She high-fived Zoe. "If I can't find a good quality one, that's definitely what we'll do."

Ms. Tobin swept into the café a few minutes later, striding up to the counter.

"Are you okay, Ms. Tobin?" Zoe asked, apprehension on her face.

"No, I am not, Zoe." Ms. Tobin glowered at them.

"What's wrong?" Lauren's heart sank. She'd been enjoying the mellower Ms. Tobin for the last few months – she hoped the older woman hadn't reverted back to her prickly former self.

"I have been interviewed by the detective!"

"You have?" Lauren and Zoe spoke together.

"Brrt?" Annie turned her head to look at Ms. Tobin. The tabby still sat at Hans' table.

"I can't believe he had the audacity to think I murdered the cupcake man!"

Lauren's eyes widened.

"Oh dear. I think you should have a hot chocolate with plenty of marshmallows to cheer yourself up." Zoe lifted a large mug.

"I don't know, Zoe." Wrinkles appeared on Ms. Tobin's brow. "I do enjoy my large latte here, and hot chocolate has a lot of sugar in it, especially if you add marshmallows."

Lauren gave her cousin a sideways glance – maybe seeking a chocolate powder with a higher cocoa content *was* a good idea.

"What about only two marshmallows?" Zoe suggested.

"I'm sure two won't hurt," Lauren said.

"Very well." Ms. Tobin inclined her head.

"And our chocolate powder has fifty percent cocoa content," Lauren added.

"I didn't know that." Ms. Tobin almost smiled. "It sounds very nice."

Phew. Ms. Tobin sounded like she was almost back to her mellower self.

Zoe steamed the milk.

"Would you like a cupcake or a Danish?" Lauren asked.

"I think I'm too upset to eat," Ms. Tobin replied. "I do have a bone to pick with you two – did you say anything to the detective about me?"

"Of course not!" Lauren stared at her in shock, the memory of Zoe writing down Ms. Tobin's name on her suspect list flashing guiltily through her mind.

"Nope." Zoe paused, the milk wand stationary. "Why would we do something like that?"

"He asked me a lot of questions," Ms. Tobin answered. "Did I like the cupcake man – Jason. Did I like his cupcakes? I never even bought cupcakes from him! Why would the detective question me? I had nothing to do with the man."

"But I thought you said you ate one and didn't like it," Zoe said slowly.

"That's true." Ms. Tobin nodded. "My friend bought some and gave me one to sample. And I told her, just as I told you girls, that I didn't care for it."

"Do you think that's why the detective interviewed you?" Lauren asked delicately. "Because he found out you didn't like Jason's cupcakes?"

"But how would he know a thing like that?" Ms. Tobin demanded. "I didn't tell many people apart from my friend who gave me the one to taste. I'm afraid I told her I didn't care for it – far too sugary sweet."

"Do you think …" Lauren paused. Perhaps she shouldn't suggest it.

"Do I think what, Lauren? Spit it out."

"Do you think it was your friend who mentioned it to the detective?" she rushed out.

"Why would my friend do such a thing?" Ms. Tobin frowned again. "How could she think I would murder the cupcake man over something like this?"

"My mother told me never to trust a smirking man." Had Ms. Tobin said that to her friend as well?

"I have no idea," Lauren said truthfully.

Slightly mollified, Ms. Tobin turned from the counter.

"Brrt?" Annie jumped off the chair and trotted over to her.

"Annie, dear, please tell me where I should sit."

"Brrt." *This way.* Annie led her to a table in the middle of the room. She hopped up on the chair opposite Ms. Tobin.

By the time Lauren brought her hot chocolate over, Ms. Tobin was smiling at the cat.

"Thank you, Lauren." Ms. Tobin studied the surface of the beverage. "You've made a swan and you have the two marshmallows as eyes – how clever."

"It was Zoe's idea."

"Thank her for me." Ms. Tobin glanced up. "I'm sorry about what I said at the counter – I'm sure you two girls wouldn't have told the detective I killed the cupcake man."

"Of course we wouldn't have – we didn't," Lauren assured her, but she couldn't help thinking of Ms. Tobin's name on Zoe's suspect list. Should she tell Zoe to strike it out?

"It must have been my friend." Ms. Tobin sighed.

"Perhaps the detective questioned her as well," Lauren suggested.

"Brrt," Annie seemed to agree.

"Now, there's a thought." Ms. Tobin picked up the teaspoon and swirled it around in the cocoa-colored foam. "I think I'll call her later this morning."

Annie stayed with Ms. Tobin for a while, then scampered back to Hans, "talking" to him for a few minutes before he left.

"I wonder what Annie's saying to him," Lauren mused as she watched the two of them.

"Maybe she's filling him in on AJ's unsuccessful training session," Zoe suggested.

More customers trickled in, until Detective Castern strode in.

"Uh-oh." Zoe nudged Lauren. "Look who's here."

"Oh, no." Lauren's stomach spun. Mitch had warned her that they might be re-questioned and it seemed that he'd been correct.

"Lauren Crenshaw?" The detective flipped open a small notebook.

"Yes?" Lauren replied.

"I spoke to you last week regarding the murder of Jason Ronford," the detective said.

"That's right."

"I need to ask you some more questions."

"Perhaps we could do it somewhere more privately?" Lauren glanced around the room, aware of the customers taking note of her conversation.

"Why don't you go out to the herb garden?" Zoe suggested. "I can handle things in here."

"And you're Zoe Crenshaw." The detective thumbed through his notes. "I remember you from last week."

"That's me." Zoe tried for a bright smile.

"I'll talk to you next."

"Okay." Zoe nodded.

Lauren led the way through the back door to the small herb garden outside, dotted with thyme and rosemary.

The detective asked her similar questions to the ones she'd answered last week: how well did she know Jason, why had he been parked outside her café, and had she been upset that he'd tried to steal her customers?

Once again, she answered each question patiently, explaining she and Zoe had gone to the town council and how the permit officer had arrived too late to speak to Jason about his illegal trading.

"Now, what about the morning of his death?" Detective Castern flipped a page of his notebook. "Apparently he parked his cupcake truck outside your cottage early Wednesday morning."

"I don't know for sure what time he got here that day." Lauren crinkled her brow. "All I know is Zoe and I noticed his truck parked outside when we started getting the café ready, which was about eight o'clock. He usually arrived around nine-thirty."

"And you didn't see or hear anything unusual outside that morning?" the detective probed.

"No." Lauren shook her head. "Not until Jessica, his ex-girlfriend, banged on the café door asking for help."

"Had you seen the murder weapon before?" he asked. "It was a tire wrench."

"No." She hadn't even noticed it when she and Zoe had seen Jason's dead body, lying inside his cupcake truck.

"That will be all for now," he eventually said, eyeing her with a grim look on his face. "But don't leave town. And don't think just because you're dating one of our detectives that you're above the law. Because you're not."

Gulp.

Lauren murmured that she understood. He requested that Zoe join him next.

"How was it?" Zoe asked as she entered the café.

"Thorough. Mitch was right about him wanting to solve the case."

Zoe's eyebrows climbed to her forehead, then she left for the herb garden.

"Brrt?" Annie looked up at Lauren from the other side of the counter.

"I'm sure everything will be fine." She tried to reassure the cat. "The detective is just asking more questions, that's all."

"Brrp," Annie said thoughtfully, before wandering over to her basket.

A short while later, Zoe rejoined her, looking a little shaken. "You were right," she muttered. "I feel like I've been totally grilled!"

"Maybe we should both have a hot chocolate," Lauren proposed, "with lots of marshmallows."

"Who cares about sugar at a time like this?"

They whipped up the treat for themselves. For once, Lauren was glad there weren't many customers.

"That hits the spot," Zoe sighed as she wiggled her feet on the stool. "No wonder Martha likes this so much."

"I could get totally hooked on this, if I let myself," Lauren admitted, staring at the little pink and white marshmallows dotting the surface of the cocoa.

"I think the sooner we buy this darker hot chocolate powder, the better," Zoe confessed. "Less sugar must be a good thing."

"Mm."

After they enjoyed their treat, more customers arrived, until the lunch rush lived up to its name.

Lauren was thankful business seemed back to normal once more. At this rate, she wouldn't have time to call Mitch until later that afternoon.

Finally, the café emptied. Annie was curled up in her basket, one ear twitching as she dozed.

"It's three o'clock already!" Zoe grinned.

"I'm going to call Mitch." Lauren dug out her phone. "And tell him about the detective questioning us this morning."

"He was scary, wasn't he?"

"That's for sure." Lauren shivered. She definitely didn't want to get on that professional's bad side.

Hearing Mitch's voice made her feel better. She told him exactly what the detective had asked her, and he said those questions were all routine, and not to worry. They arranged to have dinner that night. By the time she ended the call, Lauren was smiling.

"All good?" Zoe asked, noting her cousin's expression.

"Yes. Mitch says he doesn't think there's anything to worry about – yet." She told Zoe about her date.

"It looks like it's you and me tonight, Annie," Zoe called out to the snoozing cat.

"Brrp," came a sleepy reply.

Claire and little Molly entered a short while later, Molly looking around with interest from her seat in the stroller.

"Hi." Claire smiled at them.

"Annie!" Molly waved a chubby hand at the cat.

"Brrt!" Annie had woken up and trotted to greet the toddler.

"Cino!" Molly beamed at Annie, then Lauren and Zoe.

"I'd love a latte, please," Claire said.

"Coming right up." Zoe grinned.

Annie led the mother and daughter to a four-seater near the counter.

"How's business been?" Claire asked. There were only a couple of customers sharing a table at the rear.

"It's been good today," Lauren said. "Would you like anything to eat? We have a few cupcakes left, including my new salted caramel."

"Oh, I'd love one." Claire beamed.

"Cino!" Molly demanded. After a second, she added, "Pweese."

"Zoe is making it right now for you," Lauren assured her.

"I heard about what happened to the cupcake man," Claire told them in a low voice. "But I haven't heard that the police have arrested anyone for it."

"That's because they haven't." Lauren filled her in.

"That's dreadful." Claire looked shocked. "I can't believe the police think you or Zoe might have done it."

"What?" Molly looked up from giving Annie gentle "fairy pats."

Claire clapped a hand over her mouth.

"Thought up a new cupcake flavor they didn't like." Lauren winced as she lied to the little girl.

"Silly. Lauren and Annie cupcakes good," Molly told her with a grin. "Zoe good."

"That's right." Zoe brought the order over. "And this babycino for you is extra good, Molly."

"Yeah!" Molly's face lit up at the tiny cup crammed with pink and white marshmallows atop the milky foam, perfected with a dusting of hot chocolate powder.

"Perhaps we should talk about happier things," Claire proposed.

Zoe immediately launched into their upcoming double date at a farmers' market next weekend. "We're just waiting for Chris to text us the details."

"It sounds wonderful." Claire smiled. "Please tell me if you enjoy it. Maybe my husband and I can take Molly there one weekend."

"That's a good idea." Lauren glanced at the toddler, whose upper lip was now covered in milk foam and chocolate dust.

They enjoyed a pleasant time with the mother-daughter duo, until Claire regretfully said goodbye.

"I love coming here. Not only do you have great coffee and treats, but I also enjoy talking to you two – I get my adult conversation fix. And Molly adores

Annie – and your babycinos. I don't know what I was thinking, visiting that cupcake truck."

They assured her they felt the same way about her and Molly, and waved goodbye to them as they left the café.

"It's almost time to lock up." Zoe glanced at Lauren's white practical watch.

"I'll have to get ready for my date tonight." Lauren started tidying the counter.

"What are you going to wear?"

"My plum wrap dress." It was a key piece of her wardrobe and one that made Lauren feel good.

Once the last customer left, they quickly cleaned the café. Zoe stacked the chairs and vacuumed, while Lauren took care of the remaining dishes in the kitchen.

Annie led the way to the cottage when they were finished.

"I might be the only one watching TV tonight," Zoe joked as Annie curled up on the living room sofa.

"She's had a busy day." Lauren gazed fondly at her fur baby. "I hope it wasn't too much for her. Maybe she'd like a day off tomorrow."

"I'm sure she'll let us know." Zoe grinned.

Lauren got ready for her date. Mitch had asked her to choose, so she thought it would keep things simple if they went to their favorite bistro on the outskirts of Gold Leaf Valley. Besides, it was a work night, and they both had to get up early the next morning.

"Brrt?" Annie wandered into her room as Lauren brushed her hair in front of the mirror. The plum shade of the dress seemed to bring out the natural golden highlights in her brown hair.

"I'm having dinner with Mitch tonight," she reminded the feline. "But Zoe will be here with you."

"Brrp." Annie jumped up on the bed, turned around in a circle, and nestled on top of the pink bedspread. Her pose was relaxed, but her green eyes were alert as she watched Lauren get ready.

When Mitch arrived, Annie trotted to the front door to say hello to him, then joined Zoe in the living room.

"Have fun!" Zoe called out.

"We will," Lauren answered, smiling at Mitch.

At the restaurant, Lauren enjoyed pork with four varieties of apple, and Mitch dug into steak with mushroom sauce, while they discussed the case – or what little Mitch could share with Lauren.

"The detective is looking at everyone," he told her. "You'll know it's serious if he asks you to accompany him down to the station – but hopefully it won't get that far."

Lauren swallowed hard.

"Okay," she said faintly.

Mitch took her hand in his, his thumb stroking her palm.

"It will be okay," he promised her, his brown eyes warm.

She nodded, feeling marginally better.

By the time they were ready to order dessert, Lauren decided not to have any. All the recent sugar talk had made her a little more mindful, but she urged Mitch to choose whatever he liked. He finally settled on warm peach cobbler with whipped cream.

She couldn't resist when he offered her the first bite, but that was all she had.

Maybe she should stick to the promise she'd made herself a few months ago about getting fitter. Her dress had felt just a little tight that evening, although Mitch hadn't seemed to notice.

They talked about their upcoming double date next weekend.

"Chris sent Zoe the details before I left," Lauren told him. "We're meeting him Sunday morning at the market."

"I can pick up you and Zoe," Mitch told her.

"That would be great." Lauren smiled.

Mitch drove her home. They spent a few minutes talking in the car before he walked her up the porch steps.

"Annie might be too sleepy for spying duties tonight," she told him.

"We wouldn't want to shock her." His lips tilted up into a smile.

Lauren hoped Zoe wasn't watching as Mitch swept her into his arms and gave her a bone-melting kiss.

CHAPTER 11

The rest of the week passed uneventfully. The new sixty-five percent hot chocolate powder arrived and was declared a success – by them and their customers.

Thankfully, they didn't hear from the detective again.

"He must have realized we're innocent," Zoe proclaimed.

Ms. Tobin told them she hadn't been questioned again, either. Apparently, her friend had mentioned her name to the detective when he'd questioned her.

"This fellow is very zealous, I must say," Ms. Tobin told them. "I just hope he's not *too* zealous."

"So do we," Lauren replied with a grimace.

On Friday night they visited Mrs. Finch for craft night, filling her in on their plans to visit the farmers' market on Sunday.

"How wonderful." She smiled at them. "Is Annie accompanying you?"

Lauren and Zoe glanced at each other.

"No, I don't think so." Lauren shook her head. "I think it will be too much for her."

"She'll probably enjoy some time on her own," Zoe added. "She can play with her toys or have a big snooze."

"Brrt," Annie agreed.

On Sunday morning, Lauren gave Annie a cuddle before Mitch picked them up.

"Be good," she whispered into the velvety soft fur.

"Brrt." *You be good, too.*

"I will," Lauren promised.

By the time Mitch picked them up at nine o'clock, Annie was curled up on the sofa with her toy hedgehog.

"I hope there's not much traffic," Zoe fretted as she raced down the porch steps. "Chris says the market closes at noon."

"That will give us two hours there," Mitch said easily, smiling at Lauren.

The drive to Sacramento went smoothly, Mitch even finding a parking space quickly.

"There's Chris!" Zoe jumped out of the car and waved.

Lauren and Mitch followed Zoe as she greeted Chris.

They wandered around the market, browsing local honey, olive oil, preserves, asparagus, carrots, and rhubarb, as well as other fruits and vegetables.

Stands selling California poppies, hyacinths, and other colorful spring flowers dotted the grounds.

Lauren watched Zoe and Chris. They seemed happy together, strolling hand in hand, as Zoe urged him this way and that to check out each stand's offerings.

Lauren gazed around, wondering what to look at next. Suddenly, she froze. Was that Scott, Jason's friend? With Jessica, Jason's ex?

"What is it?" Mitch asked.

"Over there." She nodded ahead of her. "I think it's Scott."

"Scott – Jason's friend?"

"Yes."

"Hey, are you guys coming?" Zoe whirled around, her brow furrowed. "I want to check out the – what's wrong?"

Lauren tilted her head in Scott's direction.

Zoe's eyes widened. "That's—"

"Shh!" Lauren cautioned.

"What are you guys—" Chris looked at them in puzzlement.

"We're sleuthing," Zoe told him in an exaggerated whisper.

"Right now?"

"Yes!"

Zoe urged them into a huddle. "What's Scott doing here?"

"Buying fresh produce like everyone else?" Chris offered.

"I thought I saw Jessica with him," Lauren said.

"We've got to check it out!" Zoe sounded excited.

"There is nothing wrong with Scott and Jessica walking around a farmers' market," Mitch told them. "They're not committing a crime."

"No, but they are persons of interest in one," Zoe told him.

There was a pause.

"True," Mitch finally said.

"Let's bump into them," Zoe suggested. It sounded like a command.

"All right," Lauren agreed after a slight hesitation.

"You're okay with this?" Mitch asked Lauren in a low tone.

"This is one of Zoe's more sensible ideas," she whispered to him, her lips close to his ear.

"I don't even want to know what her wild ideas are," he returned in a mutter.

"No, you don't," she agreed.

"Let's do this!" Zoe grabbed Chris's hand. "We'll take the lead, and you two can be back up."

"Okay." Lauren nodded.

Mitch frowned as he laced his fingers through Lauren's.

Zoe tugged Chris in the direction of Scott and Jessica. Lauren and Mitch followed. The expression on Chris's face looked like he was trying to hide a grin.

Zoe and Chris drew alongside Scott, who was inspecting a bunch of daisies.

"But why can't you buy them for me?" Jessica asked Scott. "I know you and Jason won the lottery—"

"Scott!" Zoe affected surprise. "Hi!"

"Um – hi," Scott greeted her, looking genuinely surprised – and embarrassed. "Zoe."

"Yep, from the cat café in Gold Leaf Valley. And this is Chris. Oh, Jessica! Hi!" Zoe grinned at the girl.

"Hi." Jessica smiled at Zoe, then spotted Lauren and Mitch. "You're here too, Lauren."

"Yes." The scent of Jessica's cloying rose perfume competed with the natural scents of the flower stand.

"We're on a double date," Zoe told Jessica and Scott.

"That's nice," Jessica remarked.

There was a pause.

"Jess and I are here having a look around," Scott offered.

"I've always wanted to come here, but never found the time," Jessica added. "I was usually at Jason's on the weekends." As she mentioned her ex, she blinked back tears. "Sorry."

"It's perfectly understandable," Lauren told her.

"Yes." Zoe nodded.

"Have you bought anything yet?" Jessica dabbed at the tear that had escaped.

"Not yet," Zoe replied. "Is there a stall you guys recommend?" She looked at the cloth bag Scott held, green vegetable leaves sticking out of the top.

"The organic Swiss chard stand over there." He nodded in the direction Zoe had just come from. "It looked so good we bought some."

"We'll have to check it out." Lauren smiled at him, wondering if he and Jessica felt as awkward as she did right now.

"It was nice meeting you," Jessica said, wrapping her hand around Scott's arm. "We'd better get going."

The four of them said goodbye and watched Jessica and Scott walk ahead.

Lauren watched Jessica say something to Scott, making him turn into her body. As he did so, the bag containing the Swiss chard bumped his hip. A small piece of paper fluttered out of his jeans' pocket.

"Look!" Zoe ran forward and picked it up. She held it up as she showed Lauren, Mitch, and Chris.

"What is it?" Lauren peered over her shoulder at the fragment that looked like it measured just over one inch.

"I bet it's a clue!" Zoe's eyes sparkled.

"It looks like a torn scrap from a photo." Mitch frowned. "If we all handle it, there'll be too many fingerprints on it – although there probably are already – Zoe's, plus Scott's, if he put it in his pocket to begin with."

The picture on the fragment was pink with light yellow at the top.

"Pink and yellow. Pink and yellow." Zoe tapped the scrap against her hand.

"Show me?" Chris asked.

Zoe held it out to him.

"I've seen that somewhere recently," he said slowly.

Pink and yellow. Pink and yellow. Zoe's words beat a tattoo in Lauren's brain. Tattoo – Jason – blonde hair – pink cupcake truck.

Her mind flashed to the day Scott had helped out Jason in the truck. He'd been taking photos with an instant camera.

"I think that photo might be of Jason's cupcake truck," she said slowly.

"Of course!" Zoe tapped the sliver of photo on her head. "And I bet it matches the other piece of photo we found!"

"What other piece of photo?" Mitch frowned.

"You haven't told me about that," Chris added.

"I actually forgot about it," Lauren confessed. "Annie found it the day of the murder, but later, in the afternoon. The street had been dirty that day—"

"Yeah, really dirty," Zoe jumped in. "You know, because we had all that wind the night before? And the street sweepers ran late that morning because there was so much cleaning up to do."

"So I thought that I, or Zoe, or a customer must have walked it in, it came off a shoe, and Annie found it."

"What did you do with it?" Mitch asked.

"We saved it," Zoe told him. "I put it in my ashtray. I knew it would come in handy one day!"

"Your pottery ashtray?" Chris checked.

"Yes." Zoe beamed at him. "I also knew you were a good listener."

A small stain of crimson hit Chris's cheeks at the compliment.

"When we return home, we can see if the two scraps are from the same photo," Lauren said.

"I was going to run after Scott and tell him he'd dropped this." Zoe furrowed her brow. "But now—" she craned her head to the left and then to the right "—I can't see him."

"Maybe I should put it away for safe keeping." Mitch dug out his black leather wallet.

"But I found it," Zoe protested.

"He outranks you," Lauren murmured to her.

"But he's off-duty!"

"And I can be on-duty any second," Mitch informed her.

"Fine." Zoe handed him the photo. "But I want it back when we get home."

"Fine." Mitch nodded. "We can see if it matches the other piece of photo you found and didn't tell me – or the detective in charge of the case – about."

"But even if it matches, what does it mean?" Chris asked. "The victim's friend took some photos of him – what if the photo didn't turn out the way they thought it would, so they ripped it up so no one else could see it?"

"So why would he have a piece in his pocket?" Zoe asked. "Ooh, maybe it's

Jessica! She was in the cupcake truck the day of the murder – she's the one who found the body, and she was in our café. She could have dropped the little piece of photo without realizing it, if it was actually stuck on her shoe and not Lauren's. We didn't actually see it stuck on Lauren's shoe."

"That's true," Lauren replied.

"What we need to do is go back to your house and see if the two fragments are a match," Mitch informed them.

Zoe peered at Lauren's watch. "The market closes in thirty minutes and we haven't seen everything yet."

"We should go home now," Mitch told her.

"Maybe we could do this again next weekend," Lauren offered. "Another double date."

"Sounds good to me." Chris grinned.

"Okay." Zoe gave in.

"Does that work for you?" Lauren turned to Mitch, realizing she hadn't given him much choice in the matter. Oops.

"Yeah, it's okay." He smiled at her, making her stomach flutter.

Mitch drove them home, Chris following in his own car.

Once they arrived at Lauren's cottage, Annie ran to greet them.

"Brrt!"

"I've found a clue, Annie!" Zoe's voice was full of excitement.

"Brrt!" *Let me see!*

"This way!" Zoe led the way into the kitchen and fished around in the clay ashtray. "Here!" She brandished a torn scrap of photo.

Mitch pulled out his wallet, carefully took out the fragment Zoe had found, and placed it on the kitchen table.

"Snap!" Zoe fitted her piece next to Mitch's. "It fits – just like a jigsaw!" The two pieces showed the side of the serving hatch, the pink of the truck, and the yellow blonde of Jason's hair.

"Yeah, it does look like it could be the cupcake truck," Mitch said. "Have you got a plastic bag? I should take this in for evidence. I'll let the detective in charge of the case know about it as well."

Zoe looked mutinous while Lauren fetched a plastic bag from a drawer.

"Thanks." Mitch carefully sealed up the bag.

"Brrp." Annie sounded disappointed.

"It could be important evidence, Annie," Lauren spoke to her.

"You found something important," Zoe told the cat, bending down to stroke her. "And so did I!"

"We don't know for sure yet if it means something or not," Mitch told her.

"That guy could be perfectly innocent," Chris reminded them.

"Mmpf," Zoe muttered.

Mitch said he would take the photo scraps to the station right away.

Chris invited Zoe to lunch at Gary's Burger Diner, which she accepted. "Only if you're paying, since you're wrong about Scott."

"But if I'm right, you're paying next time," Chris replied with a smile.

"Deal," Zoe agreed.

Lauren felt like a third wheel in her own kitchen.

"Do you want me to bring you back something, Lauren?" Zoe asked.

"No thanks, I'm good," Lauren replied.

Once Zoe and Chris had left, Lauren sat down at the kitchen table, for a moment feeling abandoned. Until Annie jumped up on her lap and snuggled into her chest. She would never be alone as long as she had Annie.

CHAPTER 12

The next day, Monday, Lauren and Zoe decided to go grocery shopping and check on Mrs. Finch.

"We can tell her what happened at the farmers' market," Zoe said. She'd returned from lunch with Chris yesterday in a cheerful mood.

Mitch had called Lauren the previous afternoon apologizing for disappearing. He'd contacted the detective in charge of the case who'd been interested in the photo fragments they'd found.

"I'll make it up to you," he promised. "What about dinner Tuesday night?"

"Since most places around the small town were closed Monday, she accepted.

"Hopefully this case will be wrapped up by next weekend," he'd continued, "so when we go to the farmers' market again, we can just enjoy ourselves."

Chug chug, grr grr. The sound dragged Lauren back to the present.

She dropped her spoon at the breakfast table and turned wide eyes to Zoe.

"What?" Zoe put down the slice of whole-wheat toast she was about to bite into. "No way."

Chug chug, grr grr.

"Brrt?" Annie jumped onto the chair next to Lauren, her green eyes inquiring.

"It can't possibly be Jason." Zoe chewed her lip. "He's dead."

"Scott said he wasn't going to continue with the cupcake truck," Lauren said.

"It's not Jessica, is it?" Zoe scooted back her chair. "Let's find out!"

Lauren hurried after her, Annie by her side.

Zoe pulled open the front door and stepped out onto the porch.

"It *is* the truck!" She pointed at the gleaming pink vehicle parked outside their cottage. The van still had the gold lettering loudly proclaiming *Cupcakes*.

The engine idled, *chugging and grring* away.

"Hi!" The serving hatch opened and Scott appeared, smiling at them. He wore jeans with a leather belt and a green t-shirt.

"What – what are you doing here?" Lauren managed.

"Don't worry," he said easily, "I'm not here to sell cupcakes. I thought I'd take this thing for one more spin before I sell her."

"You've got a buyer?" Zoe asked, her eyes round.

"Nope. I'm going to take her to a dealer and get the best price I can. I was going there this morning, then I thought it wouldn't hurt to visit this place one more time. Jason raved about it."

"You mean he raved about stealing our customers." Zoe's eyes narrowed.

"Not at all." Scott shook his head. "What he did with setting up shop here wasn't great, but he genuinely seemed to like this place. He said it had a cool vibe, and it was almost as good as being in Sacramento."

"What do you mean, *almost*?" Zoe's eyes narrowed even further, until she squinted like a pirate.

"Hey, don't get mad." Scott held up his hands.

"It's nice to see you," Lauren said.

"Want to check out this rig?" Scott asked. "Hey, are you two in the market for a truck like this? You could sell your cupcakes anywhere!"

"Not at the moment," Lauren replied, thinking of her finances.

"That thing probably costs a lot," Zoe added. "But, it would be cool one day to go on the road and spread cupcake joy everywhere."

"Brrt!" Annie agreed.

"I could give you a good deal," Scott continued. "And it would save me having to drive all the way to the dealership and haggle with them. I won't rip you off, I promise."

"Well, if you put it that way …" Zoe ran down the steps.

"Zoe—" Lauren shook her head. They hadn't discussed anything like this. Who would look after the café while they plied their wares somewhere else? What about permits? She certainly didn't want to butt in on someone else's business the way Jason had with theirs. And if one of them was out on the road, how would the other cope with a busy café on their own, even if Annie helped them?

"Brrt," Annie said, brushing against her leg.

"Do you want to take a look?" She picked up Annie. "We'd better stop Zoe before she agrees to buy it in the very next second."

"Brrt!"

Lauren carried Annie over to the truck.

"Come inside, Lauren!" Zoe beckoned to her from the interior of the serving hatch. The engine was now silent – Scott must have turned it off.

The memory of finding Jason's body in there caused Lauren to hesitate. Hadn't her cousin felt the same way just now? If Zoe had, she certainly wasn't showing it.

"I think I'm good right here." Lauren stood at the rear door of the truck, which was open.

"But this set up is so cute!" Zoe grinned at her. "Look, there's a small refrigerator, and there's drawers and tiny cupboards. You could practically live in this thing!"

"Zoe's correct." Scott appeared inside the rear door, right in front of Lauren. "Why don't you and Annie come inside and check it out? No sales pitch, I promise."

"I'm certainly not in the market to buy any type of vehicle," Lauren said, before allowing curiosity to get the better of her.

"I totally understand." He smiled at her.

Wondering if she was doing the right thing, Lauren entered the truck.

The faint scent of Jessica's rose perfume flashed her back to the moment she'd seen Jason's body lying on the floor. Her stomach jittered. Annie tensed in her arms.

"I need to go outside and get some air," she muttered to Zoe, turning around to exit.

"That won't be happening." Scott stood in front of the rear door, barring her from leaving.

"Uh-oh," Zoe whispered. "Maybe this wasn't such a good idea."

"Now you think that?"

"Brrt!"

"I just can't afford to buy anything like this, Scott," Lauren said, pretending to misunderstand his meaning.

"Who cares about this stupid truck?" Scott stalked toward her and Annie. Zoe stood behind her, so close she could feel her cousin's sharp inhale of breath.

"Umm, you do?" Zoe offered.

"The sooner I dump this truck the better. I'm going to college and I'm going to be an environmental consultant and make the world a better place." His voice was fierce.

"Don't let us stop you." Lauren took a deep breath and stepped toward him. "We have to get going to the grocery store, anyway."

"Yeah." Zoe was right beside her. "It's our day off."

"I know." Scott smiled, and it wasn't a nice smile. "That's why I came here today. No witnesses."

"I knew it!" Zoe pointed her finger at him. "You did it! You killed Jason!"

"Zoe," Lauren hissed. It might not be the best time to accuse him of murder.

"Yeah, but he pushed me to do it. And I thought I'd totally gotten away with it. Until I bumped into you yesterday at the farmers' market."

"But how did you know I picked up your piece of torn up photo?" Zoe asked.

"I put my hand in my pocket to see if I had any loose change, because Jessica wanted me to buy her some daisies, and that's when I felt one of the scraps of photos in my pocket. I turned around to check I hadn't dropped any, and I saw you showing something to your friends. What else could it have been?" He scowled.

"But why would you carry a torn-up photo in your pocket?" Lauren asked.

"Brrt." *Yes.*

"I forgot about it," Scott admitted. "See, I have three pairs of the same jeans I wear all the time and five different t-shirts. I rotate them. After – Jason – I got drunk and slept it off. When I woke up, I thought I must have gotten rid of those photo scraps. Besides, what can they prove? That I took a photo of Jason and tore it up? So what?"

"That's what Chris said," Zoe muttered.

"Then Jessica called and asked me to take her to the farmers' market. Of course I wasn't going to refuse. Jessica's a great girl – except she seems to think I have money."

"But you won the lottery," Lauren said.

"Yeah, but we didn't win that much money. Jason and I went halves in the ticket, but Jason was the one in charge of it, and he's the one who collected the money. He kept saying he'd give me my half, but it never happened." Scott shook his head.

"Anyway, just before we bought a lottery ticket, I came up with this cupcake truck idea. It was a joke. But Jason had dated a woman from around here, who kept raving about your cupcakes. He decided we should operate a cupcake truck and make the cakes from box mixes and put any old stuff in them—"

Lauren's eyes widened.

"—and the ladies would buy them because Jason has – had – that special appeal to the ladies."

"Not *these* ladies," Zoe told him.

"Brrt!"

"Will you stop interrupting?" Scott glared at them. "So Jason borrowed money off my Mom to buy this piece of junk." Scott waved his hand around the interior. "Without clearing it with me first. I couldn't believe it! Mom—" his voice broke "—Mom beat cancer and had returned to work not long before he asked for the money. Mom's always had a soft spot for him – we've been friends since kindergarten, and he's always at our house. He promised to pay her back, said *his* idea was gold, and we'd make a fortune."

"Then what happened?" Lauren asked, unable to help herself.

"We won the lottery. Jason kept telling me he'd pay back Mom, and give me my share of the winnings, but he also kept saying he was busy selling cupcakes, and didn't realize how long they'd take to make, even using a mix. Then he had to drive out here, which is an hour from Sacramento—"

"We know." Zoe nodded.

"Now Mom needs the money for some more tests. She – we – thought she'd beaten it, but she's found another lump and she's worried …" his voice trailed off and he looked miserable, certainly not like a killer.

"I'm sorry." Lauren meant it.

"I dropped out of college to look after her the first time," Scott told them. "I hadn't been doing well, anyway – too much partying – so it made sense to take a break. Besides, Mom needed me. Dad works hard six days per week to provide." He cleared his throat. "Jason told me he'd paid back Mom, but it was a lie. Mom told me she hadn't received a penny from him." His eyes flashed with anger. "I couldn't believe he'd taken advantage of Mom like that – he knew she'd been sick. I confronted him that morning and told him he'd better pay Mom back that day and give me my share of the lottery money."

"What did he do?" Zoe asked.

"He laughed! Can you believe that?" Scott's face twisted. "He said he'd pay up when he was good and ready. I tore up the photo I'd taken of him with the instant camera and threw it in his face, telling him our friendship was over. That made him laugh even harder. So I grabbed the tire wrench and hit him over the head. He wasn't laughing after that," Scott said with remembered satisfaction.

"But why did you have a tire wrench here?" Zoe waved her hand to indicate the cupboards and small refrigerator.

"I told him we needed one, just in case we ever got a flat. So he bought one the day before, but just chucked it in the back here." He laughed without any humor. "I made sure to wipe my prints off it – after – after."

Lauren shivered.

"I picked up all the pieces of the photo and shoved them in my pocket. Then I got out of here. Jason wanted to get here super early that day. He thought you opened too late at nine-thirty and he'd sell tons of cupcakes to people who didn't want to wait until then."

"How did you get back to Sacramento?" Zoe asked.

"I hitched a ride in the back of a truck. They didn't even know I was lying down in the rear. When they reached the city, I got out when they parked. I don't think anybody saw me."

"Huh," Zoe said. "But you missed one piece of the photo."

"That's right." Lauren nodded. "One of us – or Jessica – tramped it into the café on our shoe. Annie found it."

"We didn't realize the significance of it until yesterday, when I picked up the fragment at the farmers' market," Zoe said. "The two fit together and we could see it was a photo of this truck."

"And some of Jason's hair," Lauren added.

"If only you hadn't picked up that piece of photo," Scott said sorrowfully. "Then I wouldn't have to kill you."

"The police have the photo fragments," Lauren said quickly.

"Yeah! If you kill us, the police will know you did it," Zoe told him.

"You're bluffing." Scott advanced toward them. "Because otherwise, why isn't that detective knocking on my door right now?"

"Because he doesn't know you're here?" Lauren offered.

"How do you know he's not at your house right now in Sacramento?" Zoe challenged him.

"Arrgh!" Scott slapped his hand to his forehead. "Stop talking! Here's what we're gonna do. You'll drive the truck." He pointed to Lauren. "And you'll ride shotgun." He pointed to Zoe.

"And what are you going to do?" Zoe asked.

"I'm going to stand behind you and make sure you two don't try any funny business."

"Brrt!" Annie sounded indignant at being overlooked.

"Three," Scott amended. "Don't worry about your cat. I'll give her to Jessica after this is over. She rarely talks about anything else since she met her – unless it's all the stuff she wants me to buy her – Jessica, I mean." His glaze slid towards Annie. "Unless she'll want me to buy stuff for the cat as well. Oh, jeez."

"Why don't you give yourself up now?" Lauren asked as gently as she could.

"Yeah," Zoe seemed to copy Lauren's tone, although it wasn't quite as soft. "I'm sure the police will understand – Jason was a piece of work."

"He was my friend." Scott glared at her. "Until – until—"

"We understand." Lauren made her voice as soothing as possible.

"Why don't we go into the café and make you an awesome latte?" Zoe proposed. "We'll even put a peacock on top of it."

"You girls are good. No wonder you have so many customers. But it's too late. I can't let you two –" he glanced at Annie "—three – go. I'm in too deep now."

"Where are we driving to?" Lauren asked.

"Somewhere deserted," he replied. "Unfortunately, there isn't another tire wrench and I don't have a gun, so I'll just have to strangle you with my bare hands. I'll make sure the cat doesn't see me do it."

Lauren shared a stricken glance with Zoe – eek!

"Purrr. Purrr. Purrr." Annie growled the sound, her fur rising.

"Why is your cat making that noise?" Scott frowned at Annie.

"Because she's scared," Lauren stroked Annie, who was still in her arms.

"Yeah. She's just heard you say you're going to kill us," Zoe said indignantly. "How do you think she's going to react?"

"The sooner this is over the better." He pointed at Lauren. "Get in the driver's seat."

"Why can't I drive?" Zoe asked. "Annie likes being held by Lauren. How is she going to drive while holding Annie?"

"Okay." Scott furrowed his brow. "But this better not be a trick." He pointed at Zoe. "You drive. Can you drive a stick?"

"Can I drive a stick?" Zoe's eyebrow raised in disbelief. "Who do you think you're talking to? Of course I can drive a stick."

"Good," Scott said in obvious relief. He unbuckled his belt and wrapped it around his wrist, pulling one end out with his other hand and stretching it tight. "No funny business or else." He held up the belt in a menacing fashion.

Lauren sucked in a breath. Her heart hammering, she slid into the passenger seat. She hoped Zoe had a plan. Or Annie. She glanced at the passenger door. It was the only thing she could think of. It didn't appear to be locked. She didn't have her phone on her, so she couldn't surreptitiously call Mitch – if Scott's eagle gaze left her alone for a couple of seconds.

Zoe tapped her arm. "Here we go," she whispered. Her gaze cut to the shift stick, then Lauren's door, then her own door.

Lauren gave the slightest nod.

"Hurry up!" Scott barked.

Zoe turned on the ignition. *Chug chug, grr grr.*

"You'd better buckle up," Scott ordered. "I don't want to get pulled over because you're not obeying the road rules."

"Okay," Zoe said. "I'm putting my seatbelt on right now." But instead of reaching for it, she quickly clunked the gear, causing the truck to lurch forward.

"Now!" Zoe shouted, opening the driver's door.

Lauren opened her own door, jumping out while holding Annie. Maybe she didn't need to investigate fitness classes after all. She flew toward the cottage, Zoe right beside her.

"Brrt!" *Hurry!*

"Come back!" Scott pounded after them.

Zoe wrenched open the front door of the cottage. Lauren hadn't locked it since she thought she would only be in the truck for a minute.

Lauren placed Annie on the ground. "Call Mitch," she urged.

"Brrt!" Annie raced to the living room, where Lauren had left her phone the night before.

Lauren helped Zoe bolt the door. They dragged a side table over to barricade themselves in.

"Is the back door locked?" Lauren asked her cousin.

"I'll check!" Zoe ran to the other end of the house. "Yes!" she called.

"Brrt, brrt," Lauren heard Annie say in a loud voice.

Furious pounding on the front door made her jump.

"I know you're in there," Scott's voice boomed. "You can't get away from me!"

"Annie?" Lauren heard Mitch's voice crackle from the living room. "What's wrong?"

"Brrt, brrt, brrt!" Annie said urgently.

"Mitch!" Lauren ran into the living room, grabbed the phone from the coffee table, and threw Annie a grateful look. "We need the police right now. Scott's the killer and he's—"

"He's at the back door now!" Zoe shouted from the kitchen.

"I'm on my way! Stay on the line," Mitch ordered.

"Okay."

Lauren and Annie joined Zoe in the kitchen. Scott pounded on the back door.

Thump. Thump. Thump.

"Quick! Let's drag the table over to the door." Lauren pulled at the heavy pine kitchen table.

Zoe joined her and they managed to shove it against the back of the door.

Zoe picked up the clay ashtray and dumped the house keys out of it.

"What are you doing?" Lauren asked.

"Scott's going to be sorry he threatened to kill us." A militant gleam appeared in Zoe's brown eyes. She hefted the piece of pottery, and walked to the window closest to the back door.

"Zoe!" Lauren's eyes widened. "What if you maim him?"

"He's trying to kill us, so fair's fair."

"You won't get away from me!" Scott's menacing voice sounded from the back door.

"Purrr. Purrr. Purrr." Annie growled the sound, her fur rising as she stood next to Lauren, her gaze focused on the back door.

"Oh, yeah?" Zoe opened the window by a couple of inches.

"The police are on their way," Lauren shouted.

"They won't get here fast enough." Scott banged on the back door.

"But this will!" Zoe threw the ashtray out of the window.

There was a thud.

"Ow!" A scream of pain. "You got me!"

"This is the second time my ashtray came in handy," Zoe said with satisfaction, turning to Lauren. She shut the window with a little bang.

"Ow," Scott whimpered from outside. "That really hurt."

"I've got another one," Zoe threatened in a loud voice. "If you don't leave right now, I'll aim the second one at your head!"

Sirens blared.

"Thank goodness." Relief swept through Lauren.

Mitch appeared at the back window. Lauren watched with admiration as he efficiently cuffed Scott and read him his rights. Two uniformed officers joined him and marched Scott around the corner of the yard.

"It's safe to unlock the door," Mitch told them.

Lauren turned the key with a click and let him in.

"Brrt!" Annie stood up straight and proud, waving her plumy tail at him.

"Thank you for calling me, Annie," Mitch said gravely. "It was very clever of you."

"Brrt." *Thank you.*

Lauren rushed into his arms for a brief second.

"Are you okay?" He scanned her expression.

"I'm fine," she replied a little shakily.

"I can't believe I just talked to a cat like that." Mitch passed a hand over his face. "And on the phone."

"Not just any cat," Lauren reminded him with a little smile.

"No," he agreed. Turning to Zoe, he asked, "Are you okay?"

"I'm fine," Zoe told him breezily. "My aim was pretty good, don't you think? Where did I hit him?"

"In the chest," Mitch said. "If the department ever has a baseball team, I'll ask them if you can play."

"Deal." Zoe grinned at him.

"What about the second ashtray you threatened Scott with?" Lauren asked her cousin. "I've never seen it."

"That was the first one I made in pottery class," Zoe explained. "It looked so horrible I didn't show it to anyone and hid it in my closet. It's a shame it didn't come in handy today. Maybe I can use it next time."

"Hopefully there won't be a next time," Lauren said with feeling.

"Brrt!"

EPILOGUE

Scott confessed to Jason's murder. Mitch informed them the next day that Scott had begged the police to keep him safe from Zoe.

"Ha!" Zoe grinned. "It looks like I won't be treating on my next date with Chris, since I was right about Scott."

"I'm sure you'll remind him about it," Mitch said drily.

"You bet!"

"What will happen to Scott now?" Lauren asked. They were all seated at a rear table in the café, twenty minutes before they were due to open.

"He'll be in prison for a while," Mitch replied.

"I feel sorry for his parents," Lauren said.

"Yeah." Zoe sobered. "Particularly his mom."

"What about the money they won in the lottery?" Lauren asked. "Will Scott get his share from Jason's estate?"

"It sounds like his mom could do with the money, especially if she's sick again," Zoe said.

"Did Scott tell you that Jason borrowed money from his mom just before they won the lottery? He hadn't paid her back before – you know," Lauren told Mitch.

"I'll look into it," Mitch promised.

"Brrt." *Good.*

Zoe's phone rang. She dug it out of her jeans' pocket and looked at the screen.

"It's Chris." She smiled.

"Do you want to take it?" Lauren asked.

"Yes." Zoe excused herself, scraping her chair back, and walked over to the other side of the room, talking into the device cheerfully.

"Still up for dinner tonight?" Mitch asked Lauren.

She'd completely forgotten their plans after the events of yesterday.

"Yes," she replied softly.

"I'm sorry you can't come with us, Annie." Mitch spoke to the silver-gray tabby, sitting at the table with them.

"They don't allow cats." He paused. "Maybe another time?"

"Brrt! *I'll hold you to that!*

The End

I hope you enjoyed reading this mystery. Sign up to my newsletter at http://www.JintyJames.com and be among the first to discover when my next book is published!

Previous Titles:

Purrs and Peril – A Norwegian Forest Cat Café Cozy Mystery – Book 1

Meow Means Murder – A Norwegian Forest Cat Café Cozy Mystery – Book 2

Whiskers and Warrants – A Norwegian Forest Cat Café Cozy Mystery – Book 3

Two Tailed Trouble – A Norwegian Forest Cat Café Cozy Mystery – Book 4

Paws and Punishment - A Norwegian Forest Cat Café Cozy Mystery – Book 5

Maddie Goodwell Series (fun witch cozies)

Spells and Spiced Latte - A Coffee Witch Cozy Mystery - Maddie Goodwell 1

Visions and Vanilla Cappuccino - A Coffee Witch Cozy Mystery - Maddie Goodwell 2

Magic and Mocha – A Coffee Witch Cozy Mystery – Maddie Goodwell 3

Enchantments and Espresso – A Coffee Witch Cozy Mystery – Maddie Goodwell 4

Familiars and French Roast - A Coffee Witch Cozy Mystery – Maddie Goodwell 5

Incantations and Iced Coffee – A Coffee Witch Cozy Mystery – Maddie Goodwell 6

Made in United States
North Haven, CT
04 August 2025